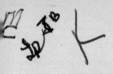

"I appreciate all your help, Adam," Janelle said, "including letting us stay in the cottage tonight."

"No problem." He pushed himself to his feet. "I'm going to call it a night. You want me to get your daughter for you?"

"If you don't mind. She's getting almost too heavy for me to carry."

Together they walked inside. Janelle stopped at Hailey's bedroom door.

"I meant to comment on the good job you're doing raising your daughter on your own," Janelle said. "She's a lovely girl."

"Thanks. She is a good kid. I'm a little worried, though, about when she gets to be a teenager. I'm sure not going to be able to give her much advice about dating and wearing makeup and stuff like that."

Janelle chuckled. "You'll figure it out." A father as devoted as Adam would do just fine as long as Hailey knew how much he loved her.

Janelle wished Rae had a father like that.

Books by Charlotte Carter

Love Inspired

Montana Hearts
Big Sky Reunion
Big Sky Family
Montana Love Letter

CHARLOTTE CARTER

A multipublished author of more than fifty romances, cozy mysteries and inspirational titles, Charlotte Carter lives in Southern California with her husband of forty-nine years and their cat, Mittens. They have two married daughters and five grandchildren. When she's not writing, Charlotte does a little stand-up comedy, "G-Rated Humor for Grownups," and teaches workshops on the craft of writing.

Montana Love Letter
Charlotte Carter

Love Inspired

Recycling programs
for this product may
not exist in your area.

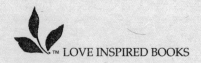 ™ LOVE INSPIRED BOOKS

ISBN-13: 978-0-373-81652-1

MONTANA LOVE LETTER

www.LoveInspiredBooks.com

Printed in U.S.A.

There are also heavenly bodies and there are earthly bodies; but the splendor of the heavenly bodies is one kind, and the splendor of the earthly bodies is another. The sun has one kind of splendor, the moon another and the stars another; and star differs from star in splendor.

—*1 Corinthians* 15:40, 41

For my husband, Chuck,
who gave me my first how-to-write-a-romance book
twenty years ago. You're my real-life hero.

Chapter One

"What do you mean, I have to pay cash?" Adam Hunter speared his grease-stained fingers through his hair. He'd taken over the Bear Lake Garage from his dad ten years ago. Adam, and his father before him, had always had a line of credit at the local bank. They'd been doing business on credit with the auto-parts store in Missoula for thirty years or more.

The lanky auto-parts delivery kid shrugged. "That's what the boss said. Only cash. No credit."

"There must be some mistake," Adam said.

"You can call Devin if you want." The kid handed him the invoice. "It says right there, cash only."

Adam took a quick glance at the papers listing the parts he knew he had ordered: a new headlight for a customer who had missed the target driving into his own garage, a dozen sets of spark plugs, radiator hoses, a couple of batteries to have on hand. He pretty much had to take the kid's word for it that the red stamp across the invoice meant what it said: CASH ONLY.

The racket of the garage's flatbed tow truck shifted his attention away from the invoice. Gears clattered and a whiff of diesel exhaust blew in through the wide-open doors as Vern Rutledge backed the truck up. An hour or so ago they'd had a call from the sheriff's office to pick up a car that had had an encounter with a deer on Highway 93, the road that ran through the town of Bear Lake en route to and from Glacier National Park, Montana.

Even from a distance, the damage to the front end of the four-door compact was obvious. Must've been some big buck that got hit.

When Vern turned off the engine, a young girl hopped down from the truck cab followed by a striking woman who moved with the grace of a dancer. Long brown hair curled past her shoulders. The afternoon sun caught the strands, touching them with a hint of red.

"Good-lookin' lady," the delivery guy said under his breath.

Adam agreed she was good-looking. Add to that, she was downright classy in the way she dressed and held herself so erect. Her outfit of slacks with sandals and a tidy blouse tucked in at her narrow waist marked her as a tourist. So did the Washington plates on her car.

"Hang on," he said to the delivery kid. "I'll get you the cash and give Devin a call later to straighten out the mix-up." The faster he took care of the delivery, the sooner he could turn his attention to his pretty new customer.

Still shaken by her violent encounter with a tree when she'd swerved to miss a deer, Janelle Townsend smoothed her hand over her daughter's hair. Thank goodness Raeanne had had her seat belt on in the backseat. Janelle had been the only one in front, and the driver's air bag had deployed on impact. As it was, Rae would have a bruise from the seat belt across her chest, and Janelle's neck already ached.

But it could have been worse.

The driver of the tow truck came around to the passenger side. His face wrinkled and weathered by more than sixty years, Vern lifted his baseball cap and scratched his thinning gray hair.

"Adam'll will be right with you, miss. He'll take good care of you."

"Thank you for bringing us here. I don't know what I would have done if that deputy sheriff hadn't come by. My cell couldn't pick up any bars."

"Yep, reception's mighty spotty around the

mountains, that's for sure." He resettled his cap. "If it's all right with you, I'll unload your car so Adam can take a close look."

"Of course. Thank you again." She eased Rae-anne out of the way of the truck. As shaken as Janelle, five-year-old Rae had a fierce death grip on her favorite stuffed animal, Ruff. The poor thing's fur had worn thin over his ears and he'd lost some of his stuffing.

"Careful you don't step in any grease spots," she said.

Although as she glanced around, she noted the garage floor was nearly spotless, certainly in comparison to some auto shops she'd visited over the course of her twenty-eight years.

At the back of the garage there was an office with a window. The man she took to be Adam, presumably the owner, handed something to the man he'd been talking to. They separated, the younger man going to his pickup and Adam walking toward Janelle.

Wearing blue overalls, he had a nice, comfortable stride and a smile curving his lips. Although his saddle-brown hair was cut fairly short, it was rumpled as though he'd recently run his fingers through it. She guessed he was in his mid- to late-thirties.

"Sounds like you didn't get a very good welcome to Bear Lake," he said in a warm, friendly baritone.

"Unfortunately, no. Particularly since I'd read that Bear Lake is the friendliest little town in Montana." She'd also spotted a billboard to that effect as they'd reached the town limits on the highway.

"Well, then, I guess we'll have to make up for that rude introduction. I'm Adam Hunter, the owner here." He glanced at Raeanne and winked. "Were you the one driving when you had the accident?"

Rae shook her head and buried her face in Janelle's hip.

Chuckling, Janelle introduced herself. "This is my daughter, Raeanne. Fortunately, we've got a while before she's old enough to drive. I was the guilty party behind the wheel, although most of the blame falls on the poor frightened animal that dashed out in front of me. I managed to swerve and miss him, but I rammed into a tree instead."

"Nice to meet you both. Those deer can be a real hazard around here. Seems like they spook and jump out at you for no reason." He nodded toward her car. "Let's take a look and see what we've got."

She followed him across the garage to the crumpled car. The front end looked as though it had been accordioned on the right side by some giant hand. Spiderwebs crisscrossed the windshield. What a mess! She'd come all this way from Seattle hoping to find a place to start over, and now what she had was a car that had been nearly totaled by a tree.

Things were not looking good for her goal of beginning a new life.

He forced open the wrenched hood of the car. Peering inside, he touched and jiggled this and that like a blind man reading Braille, humming a slightly off-key tune as he worked.

"The radiator's cracked and so is the radiator hose," he announced. "And a couple of braces are bent. Let's see underneath."

He dropped to the floor and rolled over onto his back. "The axle looks fine." Agilely, he came to his feet, all six feet of lean, muscled body. "Lots of bodywork to do, plus the windshield and the air bag will need to be replaced. I'll get you an estimate on that. The rest doesn't look too bad."

"That's a relief. How long do you think it will take to repair?"

"I've got braces and the radiator hose on hand, but I need to order the radiator and a new air bag. This being Friday and the start of the weekend, I can't get parts here until Monday. But that's okay because the bodywork is going to take several days. I use a guy in Missoula who does really fine work."

Clear back in Missoula? That had to be at least seventy miles, maybe more. She and Raeanne had stayed there last night. It was the newspaper ad for Bear Lake she'd read in the motel lobby that had brought her in this direction.

"Let me go call my body guy, and I'll get you an estimate. There're some chairs over there." He indicated a cluster of folding chairs by the far wall. "And a soda machine. Don't put any money in. Just open the door and take your pick."

"Thank you."

A car pulled up in front of the garage. A young girl who looked to be about ten hopped out. She was wearing a two-piece swimsuit that she was a few years away from filling out and had a beach towel wrapped around her shoulders. She thanked the driver and hurried inside the garage. Her blond hair hung in limp strands down her back.

"Hey, Dad, I'm home."

"I see that." Adam gave her a quick hug. "You have fun?"

"Sure. I beat some guys in my class in a race out to the swimming float."

"Good for you, Peanut." He turned toward Janelle. "Hailey, meet Mrs. Townsend and her daughter, Raeanne."

The girl had the same friendly smile as her father and sun-pinked cheeks. "Hello. Are you staying in town for a while?"

"It's looking that way," Janelle said.

"Well, if you want to go swimming, there's a

beach right near the municipal dock. Lots of kids go there."

"I'll remember that. Thank you." The July day had been more than warm under a cobalt-blue sky. Now, however, clouds were building over the mountains, threatening a summer shower.

The youngster glanced toward Janelle's battered car. "Boy, you sure hit something hard."

"It was a big tree, I'm afraid."

"I'm glad you weren't hurt bad. My dad can fix cars up like new." She shrugged as though her statement was the obvious truth, and she grinned. "He's the best."

"Hailey, you'd better go get yourself cleaned up and changed." Adam gave her a little nudge.

"Okay. See you later." She waved to Janelle and Raeanne, then jogged off, her flip-flops smacking the concrete floor with every step.

"Your daughter is cute and very outgoing," Janelle commented when the girl was out of sight.

"Yeah, I don't think she's ever met a stranger." He was still looking in the direction his daughter had vanished around the side of the garage. "Her mother was the same way up until she got sick and passed on." Residual grief laced his words.

"Oh, I'm sorry for you loss." Her own spasm of grief mixed with residual anger arrowed through her. She gritted her teeth to block the sensation.

He shrugged off her sympathy. "I'll go get that estimate now."

Janelle watched him walk away until Rae tugged on her hand. "What is it, honey?"

Raeanne pointed toward the soda machine.

"Ah, of course. Let's see what kind of sodas he has." Although she tried to watch Rae's sugar intake, today was not the day to make an issue of it. Janelle could use a little sugar boost herself. Caffeine would help, too.

Rae picked an orange soda, and Janelle selected a cola.

They settled onto the chairs, Raeanne still clasping Ruff in her arms. Cars streamed by on the road out front. The garage was a mile north of the small town of Bear Lake they had driven through in the tow truck. Janelle had noticed a whole raft of motels and a diner. A billboard they passed promoted local B and Bs. Another sign announced that the Rotary met Wednesday at noon at Sandy's Lakeside Restaurant, which featured fresh fish and steaks.

A nice little town. About as different from Seattle as any she could imagine.

Adam returned to give her the bad news about the repairs. The cost estimate was higher than she'd expected. Worse, he indicated it would be the end of next week before she got her car back.

"I can tell you were hoping for better news," he said.

"True. I'm not worried about the money. My insurance will cover most of that. But a whole week?" She shook her head in dismay. "I hate being without a car that long. Is there a car-rental place in town?"

"Afraid not. I can loan you one of mine. I keep it around for my customers who get stuck without transportation. It looks like a clunker, but I've got it running pretty good and it's insured. You can do some touring, up to Glacier National Park, come back in a few days."

"That's very thoughtful of you. Thank you. I'd appreciate that." A clunker car would be better than none. As was obvious from her three-year-old sedan, driving a luxury car had never been her thing. "But I hadn't planned on being a tourist. I was going to do some house hunting, get acquainted with this area, see if it would be a good place to settle down."

He lifted his brows. "You're planning to stay in Bear Lake? Permanently?"

"If things work out." She'd left Seattle with no particular destination in mind and a prayer that God would lead her to the right place to start a new life for herself and Raeanne.

"Well, that's great. We can always use new blood around here. I'll help you get your things out of your car and into mine. Where are you staying tonight?" He started walking toward her car.

"I have no idea. I saw lots of motels in town."

He stopped abruptly. "You don't have a reservation?" He made it sound like an accusation.

She frowned. "No. I was sure I'd arrive early enough to find a place to stay. I'm not fussy." She did, however, require clean and neat.

"Maybe not, but I think you're going to have a problem."

An uneasy feeling crept down her spine. "Why is that?"

Hailey came running back into the garage, now wearing shorts and a tank top. She'd washed her hair and it was still wet. Janelle noticed she had the innocence of childhood and wasn't yet into the awkward adolescent stage.

"We've got a big Country-Western Festival going on this weekend," Adam said. "The whole town is booked solid."

Janelle's stomach sank. "Everything? Even the B and Bs I saw advertised?"

"As far as I know. The festival's a sellout every year. Great for the tourist business."

Not so great for Janelle. "How about the next town? Maybe they'll have something?"

"Not likely. I can call the Visitor Center for you. See if they know of any vacancies." He plucked his cell from a pocket and punched in the number.

"Hey, Ariel. It's Adam. I've got a customer here looking for a room tonight. You got anything?"

He kept looking at Janelle while he listened. She noticed that his eyes were an interesting shade of gray, and there were crinkles at the corners as though he spent a fair amout of time outdoors. From the look of his physique, he probably did some hiking and camping in the woods around here.

"Thanks, Ariel. Take care." He snapped the phone closed and shook his head. "The closest available rooms are in Missoula."

Janelle's shoulders slumped. That would be at least an hour's ride in a clunker. She blew out a sigh. She didn't seem to have much of a choice.

Hailey piped up. "Dad, they could stay in our cottage."

Janelle frowned and so did Adam.

"I don't know, kiddo," Adam said. "I'm not sure—"

"Grandma put fresh sheets on the bed last time she was here," Hailey interjected, ignoring her father's objection and directing her attention to Janelle. "It's got a big bed where you could both sleep."

"That's very generous of you, but—"

"You don't want to drive all the way to Missoula, do you?" Hailey's enthusiasm was hard to squelch. "Besides, we've got our own dock and a boat we can ride in. Raeanne, would you like to stay at our house?"

Rae nodded with the same enthusiasm as Hailey, and her dark eyes glowed with excitement, the chance for a boat ride tempting her.

During the past seven months, Janelle had denied her daughter little that she wanted. But this was going too far.

"It's very sweet of you to invite us to stay, but we really can't impose on you and your father's hospitality. If your dad will loan me a car, we'll be fine."

Sliding his hands in his pockets, Adam met Hailey's pleading gaze.

"Dad, tell her it would be best if she stayed. You don't want her to drive to Missoula and have to drive back here to get her car. That would waste a lot of gas, and she's probably already tired after her accident."

Sighing, he ruffled Hailey's damp hair. "She's right. It would be a waste of time and gasoline to go to Missoula when we've got a perfectly good cottage that you can use. My dad built it for my grandmother after Grandpa died. It's small but comfortable. The kitchen's not much, but you could eat with us in the big house."

Hailey cheered. Not waiting for further conversation, she grabbed Raeanne's hand. "Come on, Rae. I'll show you where you're going to sleep."

They both went racing off, Raeanne willingly, which surprised Janelle. In the past seven months, Rae had become unusually clingy, rarely leaving Janelle's side.

"I told you Hailey has never met a stranger," Adam said, although he didn't look entirely happy about that attribute.

"You're sure it's all right?"

"Yeah, I'm sure. Let's get your gear. The big house is a few hundred feet behind the garage, and the cottage is right close to it. Dad built a boardwalk between them so Grandma wouldn't have to walk in the mud when it rained. It gave her her own private space, which she liked. I think my mother appreciated that distance, too."

Janelle imagined that too much togetherness between a woman and her mother-in-law could create a strain. Not that she'd experienced the problem firsthand. Raymond's mother had passed away before they were married. For that matter, so had her own mother, whom she still missed.

Adam popped the trunk of her car and gathered up a couple of suitcases. Janelle had no choice but to follow suit, despite feeling uncomfortable about accepting his hospitality. Especially since she found Adam attractive in an unpolished, macho kind of way. Yet he was gentle and loving with his daughter. A very engaging combination.

She had no interest in developing a relationship

with a man anytime soon, attractive or not. Fortunately, one night in a separate cottage did not make a relationship. Surely there would be motel rooms available tomorrow.

She shouldered a duffel and her laptop and picked up a bag of toys and games she'd brought along for Raeanne. With the two suitcases Adam carried, they'd have plenty for a one-night stay.

Please, Lord, let this be the right thing to do.

Chapter Two

❦

Janelle followed Adam out of the garage and down a driveway that led toward the lake. Pine, fir and cedar trees lined the gravel drive. Ferns filled low-lying spots where water collected, and there were signs of late-blooming wildflowers.

Off to the side of the driveway and visible from the garage was a swing set. Sturdily constructed yet not commercially made, the set included a slide and an exercise bar in addition to the swing. Beyond that sat a cute little playhouse no doubt designed for Hailey when she was a bit younger.

After a hundred paces, the forest thinned, revealing an extended log cabin with a sharply sloped roof. More than a vacation house, it was set so far back from the road that the traffic noise couldn't snake its way through the trees. The rustic log construction created an aura of permanence, as though the house had always been hidden there in the woods waiting to be discovered.

Off to the right, a smaller cottage of log construction appeared. It fit so well into the environment, it made her think of Little Red Riding Hood en route to Grandmother's house. Without the wolf, she hoped.

Best of all, through a break in the trees, Janelle caught a glimpse of Bear Lake streaked gold in the late-afternoon sun.

If location was everything in the real-estate business, Adam's house served as a prime example of perfect placement.

His arms loaded with suitcases, Adam pushed open the cottage door. "I warned you it was small."

"It's perfect." Grandma's cottage featured a queen-size bed the two girls were already testing for springiness, to the disadvantage of a lovely quilt appliqued with alternating pine trees and birds. A maple chest of drawers sat against the pinewood wall and a matching rocking chair sat by the window with a reading light above it. The cushion covering matched the quilt. A medium-size fan was mounted near the ceiling in one corner.

He was right about the kitchen, though. It held little more than a hot plate and a coffeepot. "I'm sure we'll be very comfortable here." Much more comfortable than a motel on a busy highway.

With a touch of her hand and shake of her head, Janelle stopped Raeanne from jumping on the bed. Hailey slowed her bouncing, as well.

"Come on, Peanut," Adam said. "Let's let Mrs. Townsend—"

"Janelle, please."

Hopping off the bed, Hailey gave the quilt a quick swipe to remove the wrinkles the girls had created.

Adam held Janelle's gaze for a moment, his gray eyes assessing her before looking back to this daughter. "Let Janelle and her daughter get unpacked. Then they can come on over to the big house." He turned to Janelle. "I'm going to grab a sandwich and get back to work. You can help yourself to whatever's in the cupboard or fridge."

"Thank you again, Adam. We really appreciate—"

He waved off her thanks, hooked his arm around Hailey's shoulders and walked out of the cottage.

She watched him go for a moment, thinking of the day she'd had, close encounters first with a sturdy tree and then with a man who seemed just as solid.

Since she only planned to stay one night, she hung a few things in the closet but didn't unpack the suitcases all the way. Raeanne put her backpack of games on the dresser and then sat on the edge of the bed to watch her.

"You ready to go see where Hailey lives?" Janelle asked.

Nodding, Raeanne headed out the door and ran down the boardwalk to the deck at the back of the main house. As though Hailey had been waiting for them, she opened the sliding glass door wide to admit them.

"Come on. Let me show you my room," Hailey said. The two girls ran off down a hallway.

The moment Janelle stepped inside, she was struck by the open floor plan. The entire living room and formal dining area filled the lake side of this wing of the house. The sliding glass door to the deck provided a panoramic view of the lake and the opposite shore. A comfortable leather couch and chairs were arranged to take advantage of the view, and the flat-screen TV was mounted between the dining and living areas. Two large wagon-wheel chandeliers hung from the high ceiling.

A coffee mug had been left on an end table, and some of Hailey's toys and books were scattered about. A lived-in room. A room where friends would be welcomed.

Adam was standing at the kitchen counter eating the last few bites of his sandwich.

"What a beautiful place you have." The space oozed potent masculinity and solid dependability, and Janelle had to remind herself that appearances could be deceiving. She'd learned that lesson too late to save herself from heartbreak. "Have you lived here long?"

He leaned against the counter. "All my life. My dad built the basic house pretty much by himself. Later, when my brother and I were older, we helped him add on another bedroom and upgrade the kitchen."

"Are your parents still living?"

"Yep. Living the good life in Arizona. Dad was having some breathing problems and arthritis. They thought the drier climate might help. Now he's playing golf, though he says his handicap is about twenty and that's for nine holes."

She chuckled. "Not quite ready for the senior pro tour yet, huh?"

"Not likely. My mother has stuck with bridge and water aerobics. They seem to keep pretty busy."

"Does your brother still live here in Montana?"

"Nope. Marc's a big-gun contractor in Phoenix. He's close enough to the folks to pop over to see them if there's a problem."

Rae and Hailey came running back into the living room. Rae wrapped her arms around Janelle's hips.

"I've got some video games. Is it okay for Rae to play them with me?" Hailey asked.

"As long as they're not violent games, it's fine with me," Janelle said.

"Trust me, they're age appropriate, though they still might be a little old for Rae," Adam assured her. "I make it a point to check ratings and ask other parents before I buy any game." He dusted the bread crumbs off his hands. "Hailey, you can offer them a snack if they're hungry, but remember, no going out on the boat on your own. You have to wait for me."

"I can drive the boat by myself," she protested.

"You can, but only when I'm with you." He hooked his arm around his daughter and gave her a squeeze. "I'll see you all about dinnertime. Bathroom's down the hall, and there are fresh towels in the cupboard."

"Thanks. You've been more than generous, letting us stay in the cottage and have the run of your home. We'll be fine," Janelle said. It really was incredibly kind of him. Trusting, too, since she was as much a stranger to him as Adam was to her.

He turned to leave, and she immediately sensed the vacuum he left behind, almost as though his leaving caused the vibrancy in the air to dim and the oxygen to be pulled from the room.

With a shake of her head, Janelle thrust such fanciful notions away.

His head filled with thoughts of Janelle, Adam went directly to his office. Something about her stirred in him a desire to protect her, keep her from harm, although he didn't think she'd appreciate his concern. She appeared perfectly competent, even calm despite her run-in with a tree.

Even so, he'd seen a hint of sadness in the depths of her brown eyes. He'd felt a connection with her, an undefined link that echoed his own sense of loneliness.

Her elemental feminine mystique called to him, as did her quiet sophistication. Chances were good she wouldn't feel the same way about him—a guitar-playing mechanic with grease stains on his hands and lube oil in his veins.

She wasn't wearing a wedding ring. Which didn't always mean a woman wasn't married. Still, he couldn't help but wonder.

Scratching the back of his head, he forcefully set aside any thought of Janelle Townsend. He had to find out what glitch had kept him from paying on credit.

Sitting at his desk, he punched in the number of Devin McCain at the auto-parts store in Missoula. While he waited for an answer, he looked out the window above his desk, past the play yard to his house, and wondered what Janelle was doing.

"McCain," his friend answered.

"It's me, Adam. What's going on, Devin? What's this about your delivery guy asking for cash only?" Adam strummed his fingers against the edge of his desk in an agitated beat.

"You tell me, Adam. I ran your credit-card number through the system like I always do, and it was declined. You overextended on your limit?"

"Not likely." He stared at the pile of invoices that needed to be paid. No more than usual, he was pretty sure. "There's gotta be some kind of glitch in the system. Did you try it a second time?"

"Three times, man. Rejected every time. You've never had trouble with credit before."

"No, I haven't." Since Lisa died, he'd barely kept up with the paperwork that she used to do so easily. But he hadn't overdrawn his account, he was sure. "Wish you'd given me the benefit of the doubt and called me. Kind of embarrassing to be told by some kid my credit's no good."

"Sorry, man. I really am. But I've got a business to run."

"Right." So did Adam. If a mix-up cut him off from his line of credit, it would be tough to keep things going smoothly. There was always a lag between buying parts for a job and getting paid by the customer. He had to find out what was going on.

"Look, Devin, we've known each other a long time. You know I'll work out whatever misunderstanding has happened. But I need you to cover me while I get things back to normal."

"I don't know..."

"A woman came in a bit ago. Her front end collided with a tree. Lots of damage. I've got most of the parts I'll need on hand, but I'm going to need a new radiator for her, a headlight and an air bag for a three-year-old Honda. Run a tab for me, will you? You know I'm good for it."

Devin sighed into the phone. "Okay. But get this credit thing straightened out fast. In this economy, my sales are way off."

"Don't worry. Just ship that stuff to me next week." Adam gave Devin the model number he needed. With a sense of relief, Adam hung up and immediately called the president of the bank in town, a man he'd known most of his life.

Paul Muskie gave him an answer he didn't want to hear. "The IRS put a lien on all your bank accounts."

That news drove Adam back in his chair. "You're kidding me." A joke, that's what it was. The Rotary guys were always pulling stunts on each other. Adam had done his share of leg-pulling over the years. "Come on, Paul. Tell me the truth. What's going on?"

Muskie was quiet for a moment. "Didn't the IRS send you a notice of the lien?"

"I don't—" He grabbed the pile of paperwork in the in-basket. His hand trembled as he sorted through the papers. He squinted trying to make out the names of companies, the return addresses.

How could he have missed a letter from the IRS? Lisa never would have.

There. A government return address. This had to be—

"You still there, Adam?"

"Yeah, I'm here." Nausea roiled his stomach. "Look, I'll get back to you. Okay?"

"Sure. Hope you can straighten out whatever's gone wrong. The IRS can sure make a mess of a man's life."

Yeah. Some guys didn't need the help of the IRS. Some guys could make a mess all on their own.

Hanging up the phone, he ripped opened the envelope and spread the letter flat on his desk. He remembered he'd had to sign for the letter when Billy Martin delivered it but he hadn't had a chance to open it right away. He'd been busy. Two customers had just arrived, one to pick up his car and the other with a fuel-pump problem and a squealing water pump. Adam must have put the IRS letter aside. Somehow it had gotten buried under the pile of invoices. And he'd never given it another thought.

Fool! He should have asked Hailey to tell him what the letter said. *A reading lesson,* he should have said.

Staring down at the typed words, the letters swam before his eyes. He rubbed his forehead.

Slowly. Laboriously, his finger moving from one word to the next, he read. *NOTICE. UNPAID. TAXES. LIEN.*

But he'd paid his taxes. It had taken him days, but he'd filled out the forms. Every one of them. Just like Lisa had always done.

You filled 'em out wrong, guitar boy!

Panic gripped him and sweat beaded his forehead. A lien on his bank accounts could mean he'd lose his business. The business his dad started forty years ago and had trusted Adam to run.

He'd have to talk to the IRS in Missoula. Figure out the mistake he'd made on the tax forms.

Admit that he'd messed up because he couldn't read. A secret that shamed him. A secret that he'd never shared with anyone outside of his parents, except for Lisa, his wife. She'd understood. And had loved him anyway.

All these years he'd been an expert at covering up his problem. Making adjustments. Working around the words he couldn't read. Joking to get past the awkward moments. Keeping his secret.

Now they'd all learn the truth.

Memories of his childhood, his humiliating school experiences, the jeers of his classmates washed over him in a hot lava flow of pain.

Adam Hunter is stupid!

He balled his hands into fists. He wasn't stupid! He could tell by the sound of an engine if a valve tappet was about to go bad. With one press of a throttle he knew if the fuel mixture was off or the fan belt was too dry and ready to crack. The guys who had given him such a hard time in school now brought their cars to him. He could run rings around any other mechanic in western Montana and Idaho combined.

But he couldn't run rings around the IRS.

Sitting on the dock beneath the shade of a cedar tree, Janelle watched Hailey teach Raeanne to skip stones across the water. Most plopped into the lake with a splash. But now and then a stone flew across the surface in two or three skips, and Raeanne lit up as if she'd won an Olympic medal. She'd been so engaged in rock skipping, she'd even left her beloved Ruff in Janelle's care.

The air was so pleasant and filled with the scent of the woods, Janelle hated to move. She couldn't remember the last time she felt this relaxed.

She checked the time. After six o'clock. Adam must be busy on a repair job.

"Hailey," she called. "If you know what your dad plans for dinner, I could get started cooking."

"It's Friday night," the child called back. "That means it's spaghetti night."

"Perfect." Standing, Janelle brushed the back of her slacks off. "You two stay close and don't go in the water. I'll start dinner." She didn't like Raeanne to eat too late or she wouldn't get to bed on time. Besides, Janelle was getting hungry herself.

While the kitchen appliances weren't new, they appeared functional, and the oak-stained cupboards made the room cozy, a place where a family would want to gather around the oak table. Colorful print pillows covered the seats of the matching chairs.

This was certainly not the kitchen of a typical bachelor, but one whose wife had lent the home her feminine touch. Janelle wondered if Adam still grieved for his wife, and thought he probably did.

Before opening the refrigerator door, she noted Hailey's third-grade report card held there by a flower magnet. Straight A's. She smiled. One smart young lady.

She found some ground meat on the top shelf of the refrigerator, a bag of lettuce in the vegetable bin along with two tomatoes. After opening several cupboards, she located a box of angel-hair pasta in a small pantry along with a jar of pasta sauce next to several boxes of cereal. A heavy iron skillet was stored under the counter.

Raeanne threw open the sliding glass door and blasted into the house, racing down the hall to the bathroom.

Janelle smiled at Hailey, who followed at a more dignified pace.

"Raeanne sure is quiet. Is she, like, slow?" Hailey's hesitant question held no negative judgment but rather concerned curiosity.

"Not at all. In fact, she's quite intelligent and used to jabber constantly. She just sort of forgot how to talk." Pressing her lips together, Janelle wondered how much she should reveal about her daughter's situation, and her own.

Hailey's forehead puckered into a frown. "Do you think she'll ever talk again?"

"Oh, yes. Given enough time she'll find her voice." Janelle prayed every night and every morning that her daughter would let go of the pain and fear and be whole again. She desperately wished she had the skill to "fix" whatever had broken in her little girl's heart and head when she'd witnessed the sudden death of her father.

"Can I help her? I'm pretty good with little kids. I always wanted a little sister, but Mom got so sick she couldn't have any more babies."

A surge of affection and sympathy for this young, outgoing, motherless child touched Janelle's heart. "Just play with her and act natural. That's the best medicine you can give her."

Raeanne skipped back into the living room. She gestured for Hailey to go back outside with her.

"Why don't you two settle down and find something on television to watch?" Janelle suggested. "Dinner won't be too long."

"I've got some board games we could play," Hailey volunteered.

With Raeanne's silent approval, the two of them raced off toward Hailey's bedroom again. Janelle had no doubt that Raeanne would sleep well tonight with all the exercise and fresh air she was enjoying.

Struck by how comfortable she felt in this house, almost as if she'd always lived here, Janelle put the meat on to brown.

But she didn't live here, she sternly reminded herself. She and her daughter were guests staying in Grandma's cottage, nothing more, and only for one night. Tomorrow they'd find another temporary place to stay. Then they'd start some serious house hunting so they'd have a home of their own.

Adam had spent the past two hours laboriously going over his tax forms. They made less sense to him now than when he'd filled them out in April.

He should've hired someone to do his taxes. But his receipts and invoices were all crammed in a box. He could barely make out what was what. Anybody else would've laughed himself silly over his record-keeping and walked away in disgust—or asked far too many questions that Adam would've had trouble answering.

Lisa, his late wife, had wanted them to keep his

problem to themselves. She was afraid he'd lose business if others knew he couldn't read.

With a headache threatening, he decided he'd call it a day. He shed his overalls and work boots and washed up in the restroom in the garage. Time to get home to fix dinner for Hailey…and his houseguests.

His steps suddenly a little lighter, he locked up the garage and walked back to the house. The temperature had cooled and birdcalls trilled through the treetops. The distant sound of a motorboat hummed across the lake.

The moment he walked into the house, he caught the scent of garlic and oregano, and his stomach rumbled. He found Janelle bending over a pot on the stove, tasting the spaghetti sauce.

"My sauce never smells that good," he said.

She jumped back from the stove and shoved a lock of her brown hair away from her forehead. With a nervous laugh, she said, "I didn't hear you come in."

"Sorry I startled you." Seeing her in his kitchen, a drying towel tucked in the waistband of her slacks for an apron, brought a lump to his throat. It had been a long time since anyone except his aging, once-a-week cleaning lady had cooked dinner for him. And she was likely to leave a tuna casserole and broccoli with cheese sauce. Not his favorites.

"I hope you don't mind that I added some spices to the sauce. I found them in the cupboard."

He sauntered farther into the room. "Of course not. But I didn't mean for you to have to cook for Hailey and me. You and Raeanne are our guests."

"I knew the girls would be getting hungry soon."

"Yeah." He took the spoon from her hand and dipped it into the simmering concoction. Blowing on the spoonful of red sauce to cool it, he sampled it. "Hmm, tastes homemade."

"I'm not exactly an Italian chef, but I do like it spiced up a bit."

They were standing so close he could see tiny golden flecks in her brown eyes. "Where are the girls?"

Her tongue peeked out and dampened the fullness of her bottom lip, leaving it shiny. "They're playing board games in Hailey's room."

"Great. Hailey gets pretty bored on her own when I work late." And he got bored and lonely during the long nights alone with no one to talk to, no one to share with, no one to care for or tell about his day.

A pan of water heating on the stove reached a full boil and bubbled over, sizzling on the burner.

Her face flushed, Janelle jumped back and lowered the flame. She wiped up the spill with a corner of her towel.

"If you're ready to eat, I'll put the spaghetti on

to cook. You can tell the girls to clean up and we'll eat in about five minutes."

Regret that the connection between them had been broken forced a sigh from his lips.

"I'll let them know."

Not that the connection mattered or was even real, he thought as he walked down the hallway. Janelle and her daughter would be gone tomorrow. The only actual relationship they had was based on a crumpled car and a cracked radiator.

Chapter Three

When Janelle had the last of the dinner dishes in the dishwasher and the leftovers in the refrigerator, she was ready to sit down to enjoy the evening.

Evidently Hailey had a different idea. She'd planted herself next to where Adam was sitting on the couch, his legs stretched out in front of him. Raeanne stood beside them.

"Dad, we promised Raeanne a ride in our boat."

"We did?"

"When we invited them to stay in the cottage. Remember? It's still light outside. Can we go now? Can we? Raeanne really, *really* wants to go for a boat ride."

Adam muttered something that resembled a groan.

"Don't feel you have to take Rae for a boat ride." Janelle stepped into the living room. "You must be tired from working all day."

He levered himself up from the couch and ruffled Hailey's hair. "Getting some fresh air is just what I need. Right, Peanut?"

Knowing she'd won an easy victory, Hailey grinned.

"Okay, everybody get a jacket. It gets cold out on the water." He looked right at Janelle. "You're coming, aren't you?"

"Why, I…" She tucked a strand of wayward hair behind her ear. "Sure. It'll be fun."

"We'll meet you down at the dock," he said.

Janelle hurried to the cabin to get jackets for herself and Raeanne, stopping only long enough to freshen her lip gloss. Although why she'd taken the time to do that wasn't something she wanted to examine too closely.

When she reached the dock, Adam presented her and Raeanne with life vests.

A sixteen-foot bowrider with an open cockpit, the boat was sleekly styled and painted red and white. The pilot and one passenger had swivel chairs. A bench along the back provided room for two or three additional passengers, and there were two cutout seats in the bow for the more adventurous or those who wanted to sunbathe.

"Do you use this for fishing or waterskiing?" Janelle asked as Adam helped her climb aboard, his hand firmly holding hers.

"More for fishing, but I don't get out as much

lately as I used to. I haven't tried waterskiing since I was a kid."

"Well, then, it's doubly nice of you to take Rae and me for a boat ride."

His lips hitched into a smile and he nodded toward Hailey. "Hard to fight that kind of pressure."

Chuckling, Janelle settled down on a bench at the back of the cockpit while the girls hovered close to Adam as he pulled away from the dock. Completely at ease, he looked very much the sea captain in charge of his vessel and all on board.

The breeze picked up, making Janelle's hair dance and whip around. As the boat speeded up, spray misted her face. The water felt cool and refreshing, the air crisp and untouched by pollution. Over the years, she'd ridden in boats on Puget Sound and on Lake Washington and had even tried her hand at waterskiing. Not too successfully, she mentally added.

But on this high-elevation lake, everything seemed clearer, the sights and sounds more distinct. She inhaled deeply and smiled. What a refreshing interlude.

After a bit, Adam let Hailey drive the boat at a modest speed. Then he asked Rae if she wanted a turn. Without a moment's hesitation, she hiked herself up on the chair and took the wheel.

A rush of love filled Janelle's chest. In this new place, Raeanne had already moved miles away from her fears and the trauma of her father's death. Her speech might not have returned, but her zest for life was definitely on the rebound.

Thank You, Lord.

When Rae's turn was over, she came racing into Janelle's arms. Her grin was as big as the quarter moon that was rising over the hills on the far side of the lake.

"You really liked driving the boat, didn't you, sweetie?"

She nodded enthusiastically.

Janelle pulled her daughter more fully into her arms. If only Rae could express herself with more than a nod or a silent gesture.

Give her time, she reminded herself. That's what the counselor had said and what she prayed for every night.

Worn out by all the excitement, Rae was asleep by the time they docked. Hailey talked Janelle into letting Rae sleep in her bed in the main house for now. When Janelle retired for the night, she or Adam could carry Rae to the cottage. That seemed reasonable. Janelle wasn't ready for bed yet, and she wanted to enjoy the night air.

Once the girls were settled in Hailey's room, Janelle relaxed in an Adirondack chair on the deck.

The clouds that had lingered over the mountains had vanished and stars were beginning to appear in the darkening sky. Bats flitted from treetop to treetop in search of a tasty morsel for their supper. On the far side of the lake, lights appeared in cabins nearly hidden by the trees.

Closer at hand, country-western music wafted across the still water.

The sliding door opened and Adam stepped outside. "Nice night," he commented.

"Hmm, perfect."

"When it gets full dark, there'll be a lot of stars. On a clear night like this when the moon's not full, the Milky Way lights up the sky."

"Seattle isn't real good for stargazing. Too many city lights and too overcast." Raised in the northwest, she'd been used to Seattle weather, but today had been gorgeous. The night even more spectacular.

He settled in the Adirondack chair next to her. "I couldn't help but notice you're not wearing a wedding ring. Are you divorced?" He spoke softly, letting his voice match the quiet hum of the breeze in the treetops.

"No. Widowed. My husband died of an aneurysm seven months ago. He collapsed in our kitchen. By the time the paramedics arrived, he was already gone." Recalling that morning tightened a knot in her chest. Although Raymond's death had been shocking, it was what she'd learned while cleaning out his desk that had stunned and hurt her the most. He'd had a mistress on almost every university campus he visited as a guest lecturer. His betrayal had cut so deeply, she wasn't sure the wounds would ever heal.

"Hey, I'm really sorry. That's tough."

Tears burned at the backs of her eyes, more for herself than for Raymond's sudden death. "Thank you." Her voice caught.

"What about your folks?" he asked. "Are they still in Seattle?"

"My father passed away when I was thirteen. My mother tried to hold things together, but I don't think she ever recovered from losing him. She died the summer before my freshman year in college." Maybe if her mother had been around and her father had lived longer, Janelle wouldn't have fallen for Raymond. Would have seen that he wouldn't be faithful.

"Losing both your parents had to be hard for you."

"Yes, it was. I felt adrift looking for an anchor."

They were both silent for a moment before Adam said, "Here comes the North Star."

She followed the direction he was pointing and cleared her throat. "Hard to miss, isn't it?"

"That's why sailors used it for navigation for centuries before the compass was invented."

"Are you into astronomy?"

"Strictly amateur, but yeah. How could I not be, living in big-sky country?"

A smile curved her lips, matching the smile she heard in his voice. "Then I guess I'd better take up astronomy."

"You're really planning to stay, then? Here in Bear Lake?"

"If I can find a house to buy at a price I can afford." She'd sold the house in Seattle and came away with more than enough for a substantial down payment on a new place. Raymond's insurance money would cover expenses for a while. "After school starts, I'll look for some sort of job, probably part-time initially."

He picked up a cluster of dry pine needles and tossed them off the deck. "What kind of work do you do?"

"I have a degree in anthropology, which is entirely useless in terms of job hunting." A degree she'd gotten because that was Raymond's specialty and he was head of the department. She'd become enamored with Professor Raymond Townsend in her first anthropology class and had been deliriously happy when he began paying extra attention to her. She should have known right then that a relationship between a professor and an undergraduate was forbidden for a reason. "But I had a couple of years of accounting before I changed my major, so I'll probably look for a bookkeeping job."

"Year-round jobs aren't real easy to find in Bear Lake. Everything's tied to the tourist trade. But I'll keep an eye out for bookkeeping jobs and let you know if I hear of anything."

"Thank you. I appreciate your help, including letting us stay in the cottage tonight."

"No problem." He pushed himself to his feet. "I'm going to call it a night. You want me to get Raeanne for you?"

"If you don't mind. She's getting almost too heavy for me to carry." She didn't want to risk leaving Rae sleeping with Hailey. There were still nights when her daughter woke up screaming with nightmares about the day her father had died.

Together they walked inside. Janelle stopped at Hailey's bedroom door.

"I meant to comment on the good job you're doing raising your daughter on your own. She's a lovely girl."

"Thanks. She is a good kid. I'm a little worried, though, about what'll happen when she gets to be a teenager. I'm sure not going to be able to give her much advice about dating and wearing makeup and stuff like that."

Janelle chuckled. "You'll figure it out." A father as devoted as Adam was would do just fine as long as Hailey knew how much he loved her.

To her deep regret, Raymond hadn't been much of a father to Raeanne. He'd been too busy on the traveling lecture circuit to pay much attention to his own daughter. Or Janelle.

If only she'd recognized the signs earlier.

Janelle woke to filtered sunlight slipping in through the sheer window curtains.

In a quick glance, she checked on Raeanne. Sound asleep, her arms curled around Ruff. As Janelle had expected, her daughter had worn herself out playing with Hailey.

After a quick shower, she towel dried her hair, dressed and went in search of something to eat in the main house.

She knocked on the sliding glass door and stepped inside. Adam was in the kitchen, dressed in jeans and a T-shirt, cooking eggs and whistling a tuneless song.

She smiled to herself. She added *can cook* to his list of attributes. "Good morning. You're an early riser."

He turned, flashing a broad smile, and a crease appeared in his cheek. How had she missed that engaging dimple yesterday?

"I wasn't sure I had anything in the house for breakfast," he said. "So I made a quick trip to the bakery." He gestured toward the kitchen table and a box of assorted muffins. "And when I heard you up and about, I went ahead and started on the eggs."

"You didn't have to go to that much trouble. We could have gone out to eat."

"Now, that wouldn't have been very hospitable of me, would it? Help yourself to some coffee." Pulling two plates out of the cupboard, he divided the eggs and put the plates on the table. "How's Raeanne?"

Janelle poured herself a mug of coffee from the pot on the counter and sat down.

"Still sleeping. I think all the fresh air is good for her." Janelle had left the cottage door open so she could hear Rae if she called her. Or, more likely, Rae would follow the sound of voices to find Janelle.

She sipped the coffee. Hot and rich, made with aromatic Columbian coffee beans, if the taste was any indication. The man was fussy about his coffee, she concluded.

"Would you mind if we ate outside on the deck?" she asked. "I need to watch for Raeanne if she wakes up."

"Sure, no problem." He put the plates, forks and his coffee mug on a tray he found in the cupboard. He'd apparently showered and shaved this morning, his saddle-brown hair neatly combed, his cheeks razor smooth.

"You get the box of muffins and we're good to go."

Outside, Janelle put the muffins on the small

table between the Adirondack chairs and sat down. Adam handed her a plate.

"I was thinking…" Sitting down beside her, Adam scooped up a forkful of scrambled eggs. "I'm going to close up shop about noon today. Some guys and I have a musical group, the lead plays banjo, and we've got a couple of guitars, bass fiddle, violin. We play country and western, and we're scheduled to perform at the municipal park this afternoon as part of the festival."

"You're a musician?" In addition to being a mechanic? And an astronomer? A regular Renaissance man.

"Mostly I just strum along with whatever the guys are playing." A slight flush colored his cheeks. "Anyway, I thought you and Raeanne might like to come along. Hailey's coming, of course. There are booths with handcrafted stuff, an art display. All kinds of food stands. You could eat lunch there."

She took a banana-nut muffin from the box and broke off a bite. "That sounds tempting. But I think my first priority is to find a motel room somewhere."

He shook his head. "That's not going to happen, at least not for tonight. I gave the Visitor Center a call again this morning. Everything's still booked solid."

She gaped at him. "Are you sure?"

"That's what Ariel told me. So I guess you're stuck here for another night."

"Stuck" wasn't how she'd describe the situation. Adam's guest cottage and house were way too comfortable for her to feel anything but very fortunate. "You really don't mind us staying?"

His lips tilted ever so slightly. "You know what they say about Bear Lake—the friendliest little town in Montana."

She responded with a smile of her own. "So I've heard." She still wasn't convinced staying in Adam's cottage was a good plan. Since they were basically strangers, it felt a little too friendly. Too much of an imposition. Still, it appeared her choices were limited. "I imagine by Sunday the town will clear out."

"Sure. Except for the regular tourists who are en route to or from Glacier National Park."

"Is Bear Lake always this busy?"

"During the summer, yeah. And pretty much during the ski season. It gets real quiet in the fall, which is my favorite time of year."

Janelle could understand that. Although spring, when wildflowers began to bloom, had always been her special favorite. She loved to dry flowers and make floral arrangements.

Adam's attention shifted to something behind Janelle. She turned and smiled at her daughter.

"Come on, sweetie. Adam bought us some

yummy muffins." Still sleepy, her hair mussed, Raeanne climbed up in Janelle's lap and buried her head in her mom's chest.

"Did you sleep okay?" Adam asked.

Raeanne eyed him cautiously and nodded.

"That's good. How about your stuffed animal? Did he sleep good, too?" Adam appeared to be doing his friendly host routine.

Raeanne looked up at Janelle in alarm. She struggled free of her grasp, slid down to the deck and raced off barefoot toward the cottage.

Adam shrugged. "She's really shy, isn't she?"

"It's more than being shy, I'm afraid." Janelle pulled her lip between her teeth. "She hasn't spoken a word since her father died. She was there when he collapsed."

"Oh, I'm sorry."

"So am I. I had her in therapy for several months, but it didn't seem to help. Which is one of the reasons why I decided to start over somewhere else."

His forehead furrowed and his eyes filled with sympathy. "That's tough."

"Yes, it is." For both of them. "I just have to have faith that, with the Lord's help and a new environment, Raeanne will find her voice again."

Adam opened the garage's big doors and went into his office.

It surprised him how much he'd liked sitting

with Janelle on the deck having breakfast together. Even with her hair wet from a shower and her face scrubbed clean, she radiated beauty and poise. And a warmth that made him want to reach out to touch her cheek, caress her soft skin.

An urge he intended to resist.

He laughed a bitter sound. What irony that he'd be attracted to a woman with a degree in anthropology when he'd barely made it through high school with straight D's.

Vern, his mechanic and tow-truck driver, ambled into the garage. His hands stuffed in the pockets of his overalls, he glanced at Janelle's car, which was still parked where he'd left it yesterday.

"Hey, boss. That lady and her little girl find someplace to stay last night? Didn't figure there'd be any rooms left in town, what with the festival 'n' all."

"They stayed in Grandma's cottage out back."

"You don't say." His pale blue eyes twinkling, he lifted his grimy baseball cap, scratched his head and resettled his cap. "Didn't know you was in the hotel business."

Adam shoved away from his desk and stood. "I couldn't very well tell them to sleep in the car."

"No, sir. That's a fact, all right. You gotta take good care of your customers. Particularly them that are real good-lookin' ladies." Vern's amused grin grated on Adam.

Scowling, Adam gestured to the Buick sitting on the lift. "Why don't you get back to work on Hardison's transmission? I promised he could pick it up by noon today."

"Sure thing, boss. If you want to keep that pretty little lady a secret, no problem. My lips are sealed. Yes, sirree." He made a zipping motion across his grinning mouth.

A muscle twitched in Adam's jaw. "Get busy, old man, or I'll tell Mama Machak at the diner that you've been bad-mouthing her chicken and dumplings all around town."

Laughing, Vern threw up his hands in surrender. "Don't do that, son. Without her weekly special of chicken and dumplings, and them pies she makes, I'd starve to death."

With a shake of his head and a grin stuck on his face, he sauntered over to the Buick.

Adam wished he could wipe that grin off, but that would be dumb. Vern was too perceptive by far, recognizing Adam enjoyed Janelle's company more than a little.

An anthropology major? Some chance he'd have with her.

At the Arthur Cummings Municipal Park near the public docks, Adam went off to find his fellow musicians while Janelle and the girls strolled through the milling crowd. They browsed booths exhibiting handmade crafts—blown glass, ceramics, quilts and jewelry. A display of exquisite handmade dolls tempted Janelle, but they were more for show than for play so she passed them by. Raeanne wasn't old enough yet to appreciate the fine craftsmanship.

Meanwhile, Adam's band wasn't on stage yet. Instead, a bluegrass band played in the gazebo, their audience seated on folding chairs in the shade of a canopy or scattered around the open grassy area on blankets. Each family group boasted a colorful picnic basket. Toddlers and young children swayed to the rhythm of the music.

The lake provided a backdrop for the event. Near the far shore, sailboats cut through the blue water, leaving a narrow wake behind them. Closer at hand, water-skiers whizzed by pulled by high-powered motorboats that carefully remained outside the roped-off swimming area.

Smoke from a barbecue floated on the breeze blowing in from the lake.

"Do you girls want to eat your lunch now?" Janelle asked. "Or do you want to wait until Hailey's dad is done playing?"

"Let's eat now," Hailey said. "Dad's friend Charlie always has them playing a long set. We'd get too hungry waiting for him to finish."

When Raeanne caught the scent of hot dogs, she tugged Janelle in the direction of the hot-dog stand sponsored by Bear Lake Community Church. A half-dozen teenagers were staffing the operation, supervised by an older woman wearing a colorful butcher apron.

Janelle ordered three hot dogs, three lemonades and bags of chips, then carried them all to a shady spot under a big oak tree where they sat down not far from the gazebo.

"Be careful, now. Don't spill on your clean blouse," she admonished Raeanne. She'd only packed enough clothes for a couple of weeks. Once she was settled somewhere, a friend would ship her the rest of their personal belongings. Until then, clothing choices were limited and access to a washer and dryer increasingly urgent.

Sitting with her legs bent beside her, Janelle took a bite of her hot dog. The bluegrass musicians, who looked to be all in their eighties or older, ended their performance to appreciative applause. As they packed up their instruments, she spotted Adam and his friends taking their place on the stand.

"Has your dad always played guitar?" Janelle asked.

"I guess so. He and his buddies play for church services sometimes."

"That's nice." Janelle had drifted away from

attending church during her marriage. Raymond hadn't been interested in religion. Now that she was on her own, finding a church was high on her to-do list. Maybe she'd join the choir, too, if she could find a sitter for Raeanne during evening practices.

But that would wait until much later, when Raeanne had regained her self-confidence and happy spirit.

The five men in Adam's group wore Western-cut shirts and jeans and had matching red bandannas tied around their necks. Stetsons completed their outfits. Adam's black hat tipped rakishly on the back of his head, giving him the look of a swaggering, country bad boy. She smiled at the image, so in contrast to his actual personality.

One of the other men cracked a few corny jokes then introduced the group: Sons of Bear Lake. The locals seemed to recognize them and sent up a cheer.

The banjo player started off with some fancy plucking, and then the violin dueled with the banjo, the two of them bowing and plucking so fast both instruments were nearly set on fire. After a long run of manic scales, they finished to the hoots, hollers and whoops of the crowd. Both men were sweating profusely.

"My goodness." Janelle laughed and put her arm

around Raeanne. "I've never heard anything like that before."

"That's Charlie Brooks on the banjo and Tiny Tim playing violin," Hailey said.

"They're great. Both of them."

Slowing the pace, the group played "Come, Come, Come to Me," a hymn familiar to Janelle. She sang along with the chorus and so did Hailey. Raeanne smiled and rocked to the beat but didn't utter a sound.

A lump the size of a boulder closed Janelle's throat, and the burn of tears stung her eyes. She'd willingly give every dime she owned if someone could erase the memory that had stolen her beautiful baby girl's voice, locking her in her silent world.

The Sons of Bear Lake performed for nearly an hour. When they'd packed up their instruments, Adam joined Janelle and the girls.

"So what did you think?" He sat on the grass and placed his guitar case next to him.

"You were all great," Janelle said. "We sang along with the songs we knew."

"Raeanne didn't," Hailey said. "She can't sing."

Adam feigned shock. "You can't sing?"

Solemn-faced, Rae shook her head.

"Well, now, that's a real shame." He opened his

case and lifted his guitar, strumming a few chords. "Say, I bet I know a song you could help me sing."

Looking unconvinced, Rae eyed his guitar.

Janelle held her breath. She didn't want Raeanne to feel pressured into talking. The therapist had told her to let speech return naturally.

"Okay, here we go." He strummed another chord and sang, "'There's a bee, a bumbly bee. He goes buzz, buzz, buzz.'"

He nodded at Rae. "Come on, I need help with the buzzing bee. 'There's a bee,'" he sang, "'a flying bumbly bee. He goes…'"

The faintest sound escaped from Raeanne's mouth. "'Buzz, buzz, buzz.'"

Paralyzed, speechless, tears sprang to Janelle's eyes. She covered her mouth so her sob wouldn't escape. Those were the first words Raeanne had spoken in seven months. For any other mother of a five-year-old, the words would mean little.

To Janelle they were an answer to a prayer.

"Atta girl!" Grinning, Adam ruffled her hair. "'There's a bee. A flying, stinging bumbly bee. He goes…'"

"'Buzz, buzz, buzz,'" Raeanne whispered.

"Okay, one more time. 'There's a bee. A flying, stinging, angry bumbly bee. I'm going to—'"

"'Buzz, buzz, buzz,'" she said, her voice stronger now.

"'Buzz, buzz, buzz away,'" Adam finished

with a flourish, shifting his gaze from Raeanne to Janelle.

Hailey grabbed Raeanne and hugged her. "You did it! You sang the song."

To Janelle, those whispered words were a gift from the Lord. A much-prayed-for beginning.

Thank you, she mouthed to Adam.

She wanted to throw her arms around him but didn't dare, afraid to make a big fuss for fear Rae would retreat into silence.

What a special man Adam was. She couldn't help but wonder if God had put that deer in her path. A path that led to Adam Hunter's door?

Chapter Four

It seemed perfectly natural for Janelle and Rae to go to church Sunday morning with Adam and his daughter. Check-in time at the motel where Janelle had made a reservation for the night wasn't until 3:00 p.m. She'd have plenty of time to pack after lunch. She'd unpacked only a few items of clothing anyway.

Bear Lake Community Church was about a half mile west of town. Built on a cleared acre of land, the one-story, whitewashed building boasted a steeple topped by a wooden cross. Dozens of vehicles, mostly SUVs and pickups, filled the gravel parking lot.

When they arrived several parishioners milled around the entrance, talking in small groups. Men greeted Adam warmly with a handshake and a friendly slap on the back. Hailey hung close to her dad, giving everyone a friendly greeting, as well.

A woman Janelle recognized from the hot-dog stand at the festival approached her.

"Hello there," she said, with a quick glance in Adam's direction. "I saw you and your daughter at the festival. I didn't realize you're a friend of Adam's."

"I'm not exactly," Janelle admitted. "I had an accident and my car was towed to his garage. Since there weren't any rooms available in town, he was kind enough to let us stay in his cottage for a couple of nights."

"Well, I'm so glad you've come to church. We're a small but friendly group. I'm Adrienne Walker, the pastor's wife."

Janelle introduced herself and Raeanne.

"Pleased to meet you. And you, young lady." She smiled at Raeanne, who was holding Janelle's hand so hard it almost hurt. "Raeanne, would you like to go into our Sunday school class with the other children?"

Rae shook her head and hid her face in the folds of Janelle's skirt.

"Rae will be fine with me," Janelle said. "Perhaps another time."

"Of course, dear. Do go on in. The service is about to begin and I must join our choir." Leaving her with a friendly smile, Adrienne hurried off.

A moment later, Janelle felt the press of Adam's hand on the small of her back, warmly possessive, as he ushered them into the sanctuary. Her breath caught, startled by how natural his gesture felt and how much she enjoyed the touch of his hand.

Like most of the men, he wore fresh jeans and a sport shirt. Hailey decided to forego Sunday school to sit with Raeanne. They found a pew near the front. Janelle entered first, followed by the girls and Adam on the aisle, the seating arrangement much like that of other families in the congregation. Except, she reminded herself, they were not one family but two small, unrelated families. Their acquaintance had been so brief, she couldn't even think of them as friends yet. Although she thought they could be, particularly since Raeanne enjoyed Hailey's company so much. Despite the five-year age difference, they got along quite well. Hailey apparently had a strong nurturing instinct.

The pastor stepped out onto the stage, and the congregation stood for the opening hymn. Like his wife, Pastor Robert Walker was in his fifties and a bit stout. Fluffy white sideburns contrasted with his shiny bald head. If he'd had a beard and red cap, he could have passed for Santa Claus's twin, his deep voice and jovial manner a match for the fictional character, as well.

Settling back in the pew, Janelle admired the stained-glass window behind the altar where the small choir sat. The scene depicted Jesus kneeling in prayer in Gethsemane.

Knowing Raeanne might get restless, she'd brought along an activity book to keep her occupied. Before long, Rae and Hailey were playing silent games of tic-tac-toe and "find the object."

By the time the service ended, Janelle felt refreshed by her communion with the Lord. This was the first church service she'd attended since Raymond's funeral, and it felt good to be back in the fold.

As they left the sanctuary and stepped out into the warm summer day, Adrienne Walker stopped her.

"I do believe that was you I heard singing, my dear. You have such a lovely soprano voice."

Janelle flushed. "Thank you."

"If you decide to stay in Bear Lake long, I do hope you'll consider joining our choir. So many of our members are getting older now and their voices are deepening. We're out of balance with too many altos and basses."

Janelle had noticed the soprano section was particularly thin. "It's kind of you to invite me. I enjoy singing but I don't have a trained voice, and I haven't sung in a choir since high school." Although she had had the lead in the student musical her senior year. "If I do stay in Bear Lake, I'll certainly consider it. Of course, I'd need a babysitter for Raeanne."

"I'm sure something could be worked out. We rehearse on Thursday evenings."

"I really don't know yet what my plans will be." Nor did she know when she'd feel comfortable again leaving Rae with a sitter.

"Keep us in mind, dear, if things work out." With that, Adrienne scooted off to speak with another member of the congregation.

"Come on, Rae," Hailey said. "I'll race you to the truck." The two of them dashed off as though they'd just escaped from solitary confinement.

"Watch out for cars!" Janelle called after them, but they were already on their way, galloping across the parking lot.

"They'll be fine." With his hand at her back, Adam nudged her toward his truck. "I'd say the pastor's wife intends to hog-tie you and drag you into the choir whether you want to go or not."

"I think a pastor's wife must be required to take a class in recruiting volunteers for church functions."

"In that case, I'd guess she got an A plus."

Janelle laughed. "The truth is, assuming I stay here in Bear Lake, I would like to sing in the choir. But I haven't left Raeanne alone since—"

"Since your husband died?"

She nodded.

"I understand. It's hard to adjust after you lose someone you love."

Even harder when it turned out the one you loved didn't love you in return. Certainly not exclusively.

After a quick lunch, Adam went into the garage and sat down at his desk. He had to figure out this tax business before things got any worse. And they would get worse. He'd finally deciphered the letter from the IRS. He was expected to appear at a hearing just weeks away.

Chances were good that if he didn't have some answers by then the lien on the bank account would be the least of his worries. He'd be behind bars.

He got out the paperwork and turned on his computer, pulling up his tax return. For a moment he stared at the monitor. The numbers swam across the screen like minnows fleeing a largemouth bass.

He blinked and knuckled his eyes. When he looked again, the image of Janelle appeared superimposed over the tax return. Smiling at him. Her lips slightly parted. A hint of laughter in her eyes.

An ache tightened in his chest, and a rush of wanting caught him by surprise.

Shaking off the sensation, he chided himself for even thinking about Janelle. He had the IRS to worry about. The fact that she and her daughter seemed to fit so perfectly with him and

Hailey wasn't worth considering. He barely knew the woman. She had her own issues to work out, needed to make a home for her daughter. Needed to start over clean.

No way would she want to get tangled up in his life.

Gritting his teeth, he forced himself to drag out the stack of invoices from last year and his bank records. He'd start over, too. If he concentrated hard enough, he'd get it right this time. He picked up a pencil and found a lined notepad.

He wasn't a stupid guy. He could do this.

Immediately his palms began to sweat. His fingers cramped around the pencil. Pain crept up the back of his neck. Just like it always had when he'd taken tests in school.

But this time he couldn't fake the answers.

There was no question. He needed help.

He could take this pile of gibberish to one of the Rotary guys who was a CPA, but then he'd have to explain why he couldn't handle his own record-keeping.

There were probably lots of accountants in Missoula or even Kalispell who could do the job for a fee. But in many ways, western Montana was one small community. Word would get back to Bear Lake.

The heat of shame rose up his neck. He'd worked so hard, so many years, to keep his secret.

Somehow he'd have to do it himself.

He didn't know how long he'd struggled trying to make sense of his records when he heard a light rapping on his open office door. He looked up to find Janelle smiling at him.

"I've packed up our things and put them in your loaner car, so we're about to leave. It's almost three. We can check into the motel now."

"Oh, yeah." He spun his chair around and stood. He tossed his pencil on the pile of invoices. Janelle was leaving and suddenly he didn't want her to go. "I guess you'll need the key, won't you."

Her lips twitched. "I imagine it goes faster with the engine turned on."

"You could always ask Rae to push while you steer."

She laughed. "I'm sure she'd be willing to try, but I don't think we'd get very far." Her gaze skipped to his cluttered desk and the mess he'd made of things. "Looks like you're having a bad bookkeeping day."

"Yeah, I am." He tucked his fingertips into the pockets of his jeans. He didn't think he'd ever had a *good* bookkeeping day. "Numbers just aren't my thing. They make me crazy."

"Is there something I can help you with? We don't have to be at the motel right at three o'clock."

"No, that's—" He mentally stepped on the brakes. He had a problem and needed help. Janelle needed a part-time job and a place to stay while she house hunted. Maybe, just maybe...

He shifted his weight from one foot to the other. "Look, I just had an idea. I'm sort of in trouble with the IRS. I messed up my tax return, I guess." Big-time! "Maybe we could help each other out. You stay in the cottage for as long as you need to while you're house hunting, and in your spare time you can straighten out the mess I've made with my taxes. I could pay you whatever you think is right."

Janelle's jaw dropped. He was offering her a place to stay and a job?

"I...I don't know." Her gaze fell on his desk. A chaos of paperwork covered the top, and one drawer was so full it couldn't be closed. On some level that much disorder offended her sensibilities, and her fingers itched to straighten out the mess. Fix it.

"You and Rae would be a lot more comfortable here than at the Pine Tree Inn," he pointed out. "Not that it's a bad motel. But here you have the run of the house. The lake's right at your doorstep." He shrugged as if it should be the easiest decision in the world.

It should be, except that staying in such close proximity to Adam was far too tempting. "Isn't there an accountant here in town?"

"Sure there is." He took a couple of steps toward her. His eyes looked tired, his hair mussed.

"Except I don't like everyone in town to know my business. You seem like someone who could keep stuff confidential."

She sensed there was more to his story than he was telling. "Just how much trouble are you in with the IRS?"

He shifted his gaze to a couple of cars in the garage that were waiting for repair and cleared his throat. "They've put a lien on my bank accounts. There's a hearing in a couple of weeks. If I don't have my books in order by then…"

He left the thought hanging, but Janelle knew that it would mean big problems for him. With fines and penalties, the problems could be big enough to bankrupt him. She wondered how he'd gotten himself into such a deep hole.

"I only took one class in tax accounting in college, and that was years ago. Beyond that, I've done the family taxes and my husband's business returns." She eyed the paper maze on the desk again. Would she even be able to find the bottom of the pile? "I'm not all that experienced if you've got a complicated return."

He brought his gaze back to hers. "There are a couple of schedules for the business. Not much else. It shouldn't be that hard. I've got one of those computer programs that's supposed to do all the adding and stuff."

Then why couldn't he do it himself? Because

he'd established no sense of order? Or was he simply averse to dealing with the IRS?

She worried a loose button on her blouse, trying to think what she should do. Free rent for a month or two plus a little cash would help her stretch her funds. She already knew Rae didn't want to leave Hailey; she'd become quite attached to the girl in just two days. So had Janelle, for that matter.

And she would enjoy the challenge of putting things right in Adam's financial world.

But the real kicker, the thing that made Janelle want to agree to stay the most, was that Adam had an uncanny way of getting Raeanne to relax. To be herself. To speak, however haltingly. How could she walk away from that?

She took a deep breath. "All right, I'll stay."

"Great!" The strain around his eyes and the tightness of his shoulders visibly eased.

"Tomorrow you can show me what you've got. If it's too complex a tax return for me to handle, I'll tell you." Or if it would be better to light the desk on fire and start over. "Then you'd have to find someone else. I have no desire to get you into more trouble with the IRS than you're already in because of my inexperience."

"It's a deal."

He extended his hand and she took it. His palm was rough and calloused, his grip firm. His smile reached his eyes, crinkling the corners. His dimple appeared and she couldn't help but wonder where this *deal* would lead them.

By Monday afternoon, Janelle realized she had a serious challenge on her hands. Two of Adam's tax returns were being questioned by the IRS. Numbers didn't match. Business expenses were twice what they had been three years ago. Income was down, expenses up.

He'd paid some taxes, but on the surface it appeared not nearly enough.

Unless she could justify the income vs. expenses.

Considering the number of cars and trucks that had been brought into the shop this morning, Adam's garage was a thriving business, but his record-keeping was a disaster.

Bills and receipts weren't separated. She dug around in the stack of paperwork on his desk for the better part of an hour to come up with all the monthly bank statements. Little wonder the IRS questioned his returns.

She looked up when he stepped into the office. He stood in the doorway a moment, wiping his hands with a blue cloth, looking amazingly macho in his overalls. Her late husband had always been well-groomed, most often wearing a tie and a sport coat, his hair carefully styled. She wondered why she'd thought his appearance had been so important when Adam's more earthy look now seemed so much more virile.

"How's it going?" he asked.

Mentally, she pushed her inappropriate thoughts aside. "Clearly there are some—" she searched for a diplomatic word that wouldn't offend him "—inconsistencies in the recent tax returns. I'm going to have to go back three years and re-create that tax return, which looks okay, then move forward through the next two years."

"Big project, huh?"

"It's going to take a while, I'm afraid. I'd like to reorganize pretty much everything and start fresh."

Looking down, he scuffed the toe of his work boot on the concrete floor. "I really botched things, didn't I?"

"Tax returns can be tricky." Particularly for a man who worked with his hands and lacked a talent for record-keeping. She suspected his late wife handled the latter for both the garage and household. Her passing away had put him in a bad spot, not only emotionally but at a practical level for someone running a business.

"Dad! Dad!" Hailey, closely followed by Raeanne, raced full speed into the garage. "Can we go swimming at the lake? Can we?"

"Slow down, young lady. Who is *we?* And where are you going?"

Hailey shot a glance in Janelle's direction. "Rae wants to go swimming, and we thought maybe her mom could take us there."

Janelle's lips twitched. "It's Rae's idea to go swimming?"

"Well, no." Her cheeks coloring, Hailey checked with her dad. "But I asked her and she nodded yes."

"You know what?" Janelle straightened the pile of papers on the desk as best she could. "I think I could use a break. A picnic lunch and a swim would be a perfect way to spend the afternoon."

Hailey cheered and Rae grinned.

"If it's all right with your father," Janelle added.

"Sure." He shrugged. "Sounds like a good way to keep this demanding duo out of my hair."

Hailey threw herself at her father and hugged him. "Thank you, Daddy."

Janelle smiled at the obvious love Adam and his daughter shared. Her own father had been mostly an absentee dad before his death. She hadn't had a chance to develop such a close bond as Hailey and Adam had.

Her chest suddenly ached with regret. Raeanne hadn't had much of chance with Raymond, either. And now there was no chance at all.

The following morning, Janelle decided she couldn't delay her search for a house any longer.

As comfortable as both she and Raeanne felt living in Adam's cottage, she wanted to be settled by the time Rae started school at the end of August.

Granted, she'd done some preliminary searching on her laptop for homes in the area. But that wasn't the same as actually seeing the real estate.

She'd house hunt in the mornings and work on Adam's tax returns in the afternoon.

He gave her the name of a Realtor, and she called ahead for an appointment. Despite Janelle's warning that they might get bored, the girls insisted they come with her.

Lake Country Realty was located on the main highway just south of town. It occupied a small log cabin with pictures of houses and properties for sale featured on a bulletin board by the front door.

Janelle opened the door and herded the girls inside.

A slender woman in her forties, dressed in casual slacks and a jacket, met them with a welcoming smile.

"Hello there, you must be Ms. Townsend." She nodded to the girls. "I'm Sharon Brevik. We talked earlier."

Janelle introduced Raeanne. "You may already know Adam Hunter's daughter, Hailey. We're staying at his cottage while he's repairing my car."

Sharon said hello to the girls. "I've known Adam forever. Best mechanic around and a genuinely nice guy." The slight lift of her brows suggested she was more than a little curious to know if there was something going on between Janelle and Adam other than car repairs.

"Yes, he does seem to be all of that. He recommended I see you about buying a house."

"Perfect. Let's get started."

They all sat around Sharon's desk, which was covered with for-sale flyers, escrow papers and who knew what else. On the one clear corner of the desk sat a photo of Sharon and her family.

She began by asking what sort of house Janelle was looking for and her price range.

After they spoke for a while, Sharon said, "Since you're not familiar with the area, why don't I take you on an orientation tour? We'll drive by some houses that are currently for sale and I'll tell you about the neighborhood, where the schools are and so on."

Nearly three hours later, the girls were beginning to squirm in the backseat of Sharon's car. Janelle was developing a headache. They'd driven through the upper lake district, along the east shore, as far south as Polson and back to Bear Lake, while skirting the Indian reservation and national forest land. Finally they returned to Lake Country Realty.

The girls couldn't wait to get out of the car. Neither could Janelle.

"You've given me a lot to think about," she told Sharon. "I'm going to have to get the girls some lunch then think about this."

"Call me whenever you want to narrow down the choices."

Janelle agreed, then took the girls to the Pee Wee Drive-In and got them all burgers and shakes. It was not generally her preference for healthy eating, but the girls had been so well behaved that she felt they deserved a treat.

Back at Adam's house, while the girls decided to eat down by the dock, she went directly inside and collapsed on his leather couch.

A few minutes later, she heard the sliding door open.

"You were gone a long time."

At the sound of Adam's voice, she opened one eye. His mechanic's overalls had picked up a grease stain on the right shoulder. "Do you have any idea how many thousands of acres the greater Bear Lake area covers?"

One side of his mouth hitched into a grin. "Generally speaking, yeah."

"How am I ever going to decide where I'd like to live, even assuming there's a house for sale that I like and can afford?"

"You're smart. You'll figure it out." He sat down beside her. "Turn around. I'll give you a massage."

She groaned with pleasure as his thumbs worked

at the knotted muscles of her shoulders and neck, kneading in just the right spots. This was worth even more than free rent and a part-time job combined.

It was also something she shouldn't get used to. Not when their arrangement was only temporary.

Chapter Five

As Janelle was fixing dinner, she noticed the quiet. No TV on. No giggles from Hailey's bedroom. And when she looked out toward the dock, no sign of the girls. Thankfully, Adam's boat was still tied to the dock, so Hailey hadn't decided to take it out for a clandestine ride.

Even so, her stomach twisted on a mother's fear. Where could they have gone? Hailey had come into the house a half hour ago, got something from a cupboard and hurried back outside without even saying hello.

She dried her hands on a paper towel. They couldn't have gone far. She'd check first with Adam. Hailey was good about keeping her father informed of her whereabouts. She hoped.

In the garage she found both Adam and Vern with their heads under the hood of an SUV.

"Adam? Do you know where Hailey is?"

He backed out from under the hood, frowning. A streak of grease marked his cheek. "No. Why? Is something wrong?"

"I've just lost track of the girls. I'm sure they're fine." Still, Raeanne had been so clingy since her father's death. Now Janelle felt her daughter's absence like a part of herself had gone missing. Maybe it was Janelle who had become the clingy one.

Adam said something to Vern and then walked over to Janelle. He didn't look concerned. "She's probably close by. I just saw them a minute or so ago. Let's take a look."

His lack of concern didn't assuage her feelings of unease.

They stepped out of the garage into slanted rays of sunlight filtering through the forest treetops. Dust motes and flying insects floated through the columns of light. The warm air held the scent of pine trees and summer-dry grass.

"You checked down by the dock?" he asked.

"I didn't see them there, and the boat was still tied up at the dock. Would Hailey walk to a friend's house or as far away as the park?" Hailey might be old enough to be on her own in familiar territory, but Raeanne could get lost. Or be picked up by a stranger.

Butterfly wings of panic fluttered in Janelle's chest. *Don't buy trouble!*

"She'd tell me if she was going that far." He stood still, listening. So did Janelle.

As though carried on the breeze caressing the treetops, Janelle heard Hailey's distinctive giggle.

"They're that way." Adam pointed through the woods and headed in that direction.

Between pine trees, firs and an occasional rock outcropping, it was impossible to walk a straight line for more than a few feet. Pine needles and downed branches covered the forest floor. In sunny spots, late-blooming wildflowers peeked up through cracks between rocks or in tiny meadows. Janelle made a mental note to pick some flowers to dry one day soon.

They found the girls sitting in a natural circle of rocks. Adam held out his hand to stop Janelle from racing over to them.

With a twinkle in his eyes, he put his finger to his lips. "Let's watch a minute."

Puzzled, Janelle kept her eye on Raeanne. Suddenly, a small creature jumped in the air after a slender twig Rae had twirled above it. A squirrel? They could carry diseases. Rae shouldn't be—

Before she completed the thought, she realized she had been wrong.

"A kitten," she whispered, relieved but puzzled where the girls had found it.

"Looks like. Sometimes people dump unwanted cats in the woods around here thinking they'll learn how to forage for themselves. Most times, before they figure it out, a fox or a wolf will get them."

Janelle cringed. "How cruel."

"Not from the fox's or wolf's perspective. It's the humans who are the cruel ones. They ought to know better."

"I agree."

Adam strolled up to the girls. "Hey, it looks like you found a baby mountain lion."

Both girls whirled, eyes wide and mouths open.

"He's just teasing you, girls." Janelle knelt beside Raeanne. The short-haired kitten with black, white and orange calico markings looked to be no more than seven or eight weeks old, barely weaned. She petted its little head. "Where did you find her?"

Hailey looked up at her father. "She was playing too close to the highway. I was afraid she'd get run over."

Adam hunkered down next to Hailey. "And you thought she might be hungry, which is why you snitched a can of tuna from the cupboard without telling anyone what you were doing." His gaze fell on the tin can in the middle of the rock circle.

Hailey's blue eyes pleaded with him for understanding. "She's awful skinny."

"Yeah, I can see that." He gave Hailey's ear a gentle tweak. "So what are you going to do with her?"

"I thought maybe…" She glanced at Raeanne. "I thought Raeanne would like to keep her."

Janelle choked on a laugh. The child had cleverly decided her father wouldn't deny Raeanne a kitten even if he might have told his daughter no.

Raeanne tugged on Janelle's shirtsleeve and turned her big brown, serious eyes on her.

"You want to keep the kitty?"

Raeanne nodded vigorously.

"Are you two sure the kitten doesn't belong to someone who lives around here?"

Both girls nodded their heads. "We're sure," Hailey said.

"Well, then…" She checked with Adam, who shrugged, indicating it was her choice. "There are lots of animals around here who could hurt the kitty, so she'll have to be an indoor cat."

Smiles bloomed on both young faces.

"Raeanne, you know if it's your cat, you'll have to take care of her." Rae appeared not only agreeable but tickled at the prospect.

Janelle tried to think of an argument why having a kitten wouldn't be a good idea and failed to find one. Having a live animal to love and care for would give Rae some responsibility. Hopefully a pet would help her to feel "normal."

She cupped Raeanne's cheek and smiled. "So what are you going to name your cat?"

In a soft but very clear voice, Rae said, "Kitty Cat."

Pressing her lips together to halt the tears that threatened, Janelle said, "I think Kitty Cat is a perfect name."

Even more precious was the rare sound of her daughter's voice.

It was decided Kitty Cat would stay in the cottage at night, which seemed to suit her just fine. She quickly claimed the middle of the bed between Janelle's and Rae's feet as her special spot. In the daytime she'd have the run of the main house and likely the undivided attention of two little girls.

An early trip to the local veterinarian the next morning proved the kitten was healthy. A stop at the general store provided the necessities, including kitty kibble, a feeding dish and a litter box. The girls added two little balls that jiggled when they rolled across the floor and a mechanical mouse for Kitty Cat's playtime toys.

When Adam came in for dinner that evening, he plucked a handful of red grapes from the bowl Janelle had set on the kitchen counter.

"I've got my Rotary meeting tomorrow at lunchtime." He popped a grape into his mouth. "I usually take Hailey to Mrs. Murphy's house—"

"Oh, Daddy, I don't want to go to Mrs. Murphy's," Hailey complained from the living room, where she and Raeanne were watching TV and playing with the kitten. "There's nothing to do there."

"Or," he emphasized, "she visits a friend's house for a couple of hours."

"Why can't I stay here with Rae and her mom?"

"Because Janelle has other things to do besides babysit you?"

Janelle wiped her hands on a tea towel. "It's all right. I can skip a day of house hunting. Maybe we girls can do something together." She had to think for a moment just what that would be. Bear Lake didn't exactly have a lot of attractions like museums or amusement parks for kids to enjoy.

"Is there a library in town?" Janelle liked to have a variety of books to read to Raeanne. By now she'd pretty well memorized all the books they had brought from Seattle.

Adam's eyes flared for a moment, a quick flash of surprise. Or panic? Janelle couldn't be sure which or why the mention of the library would get such a strange reaction from him.

"Yeah, we've got a library. It's not very big, but you can order any books you want from the main county library."

"Well, then, we can spend some time at the library and maybe have a picnic lunch somewhere."

Adam checked with his daughter. "You okay with that, Peanut?"

"Sure." She wrinkled her nose. "It's better than Mrs. Murphy's."

Janelle smiled at Hailey, who sometimes acted like a ten-year-old going on sixteen. Adam was sure to run into some rocky moments when his daughter became a teenager, but with patience—and a lot of prayers—the two of them ought to get along fine.

Twisting the tea towel into a knot, she glanced away from the two girls. Both of them were minus a parent, a parent who could temper their partner's over-the-top reactions to adolescent behavior or bolster discipline when needed. Parenting a teenager alone, she was sure, would be a tightrope act with no safety net.

A demanding feat both she and Adam would face all too soon and on their own.

Glancing away from the girls, Janelle sternly reminded herself that even if Raymond had lived she still would have carried most of the burden of raising Raeanne.

The upstairs banquet room of Sandy's Lakeside Restaurant, as the billboard at the edge of town announced, served as the weekly meeting place for the Bear Lake Rotary.

Adam took the stairs two at a time. He'd been delayed at the garage by a customer who knew nothing about transmissions, including why his car no longer went in Reverse.

When the customer finally left, he'd hurriedly changed into good jeans and a sport shirt. Now he had to rush not to be late to the meeting or it would cost him a buck plus a serious razzing from his Rotary buddies.

"You just made it under the wire." Charlie Brooks, the banjo player from their country-western group, greeted him at the door. A tall, wiry guy, he owned the local Laundromat and did beautiful cabinetry work. "Maybe since you cut this so close, you'd like to make a contribution to our health-and-welfare fund." He held out a bright red bucket and rattled the change inside.

"No thanks. I'm saving up till our honorable president hits me with a really big fine for forgetting my badge." He touched the badge clipped to his shirt pocket just to make sure it hadn't fallen off.

Joshua Higgins, said honorable president, banged his gavel on the rostrum. "We'll come to order now. Clarence, quit telling Max your fish stories and get over here and lead the flag salute."

The group of about thirty members laughed.

With a maximum of fussing and shoulder bumping, they quieted down for the flag salute, followed by Pastor Walker's invocation.

Adam sat next to Charlie. The salads and bread baskets were already on the table. The guys, plus two female members, started eating while Joshua asked for announcements.

Brad Steely confessed that his daughter was getting married, which brought cheers and cost him five bucks that he dropped in the bucket. Owen Marcus was coerced into revealing he'd caught a five-pound lake trout; he paid two dollars a pound into the health-and-welfare fund.

Adam had known most of these men the better part of his life. Bear Lake and the environs was a pretty tight-knit community, and the locals tended to help each other when there was a need. He counted them all as his friends.

Despite the fact that the restaurant specialized in steaks and fish, a waitress delivered this week's chicken covered with mystery sauce over rice and vegetables on the side. Today it smelled of curry.

Not particular about what he ate, Adam sliced off a bite of chicken. While it wasn't his idea of gourmet, it would do for lunch. Though he had to admit he'd come to prefer the spices Janelle added to even a simple dish like baked chicken.

When most of the members had finished their main course, Joshua stood again. "We've got two things coming up, folks. First up is the Labor Day pancake breakfast to benefit the volunteer fire department. How many cooks have we got?"

Adam, among several others, raised his hand, and the breakfast committee chairman wrote down their names.

"We're fast coming up on elections," Joshua continued. "I want a full slate of officers, so you can expect to be arm-twisted one way or another."

Everyone groaned, and Charlie nudged Adam with his elbow. "You know, you'd make a great president. Everybody likes you. You've been in the club a long time. You ought to think about running."

Panic, like a freight train, roared through Adam's head. His fork nearly slipped from his fingers and beads of sweat formed on his forehead.

"Nah, not me." His throat felt as if someone had tightened a wrench around it. "I don't have time for all that busywork and stuff Joshua has to do."

Charlie gave him a disappointed look. "Man, you've got as much time as anybody else in this outfit. Besides, we need some younger guys to take over instead of all these gray heads."

Adam could barely draw a breath. The chicken and curry threatened to rebel in his stomach. His eyes darted side to side in search of an exit. A quick escape. A place to hide. A way to keep his secret.

"You're so smart, why don't you volunteer to be

president? That Laundromat of yours takes care of itself. All you do is collect the quarters and take 'em to the bank. You got lots of time on your hands."

"Ha! If you had four kids to raise on your own, you wouldn't say that." Charlie shook his head. "You're just chicken to stand up there without a guitar in your hands."

The problem was more than mike fright. It was all those other things a president had to do—read announcements, write letters to other clubs, make reports to the national Rotary. No way could Adam do any of that.

No way did he want the entire Rotary Club membership to discover he couldn't.

Business finished and a chocolate pudding was served for dessert. The president moved on to the day's speaker, a well-known fishing and hunting guide in the area. Adam barely heard a word the man said. And when he was finished with his talk, Adam was the first one out the door.

Nobody was going to arm-twist him into doing something that would reveal his shame.

After visiting the library and picking out books, Janelle found a quiet meadow off of a gravel road where she and the girls could have their picnic.

In a shady spot, she spread an old blanket on the ground, one she always kept in her trunk for impromptu picnics or emergencies. Hailey carried Adam's ice chest that Janelle had filled with sandwiches, chips, soft drinks and cookies from the bakery in town.

Janelle sat down, bending her legs sideways. "This is nice, isn't it?" At midday, the meadow was quiet with only a slight breeze whispering through the tops of the pine trees that surrounded the clearing.

Hailey plopped herself down on the blanket. "I remember when I was little my mom and dad used to take me on picnics. Sometimes we'd hike to a lake and Dad would fish from the shore." Her wistful tone clearly indicated she missed her mother and the days they'd shared as a family.

"Did your mother like to fish, too?" Janelle handed each of the girls a sandwich.

"Not very much. But she liked being outdoors, I think."

"Probably very much liked spending a few hours with you and your dad."

"I guess." With a decided lack of enthusiasm and a great deal of nostalgia, Hailey took a bite of her sandwich. "Dad says she's up in heaven watching over us. Do you think that's true?"

Scooting closer to the child, Janelle put her arm around Hailey. "Absolutely. I know your mother loved you very much and would have done everything in her power to stay here on earth with you. But for some reason we can't understand, God called her to heaven to be with Him. But that hasn't stopped her from loving you. She's still right here in your heart."

Her chest aching for Hailey's grief, Janelle placed her hand over Hailey's heart. "She'll always be there with you."

Rae slid over to sit on the other side of Hailey and put her arm around her new friend. She rested her head on Hailey's shoulder.

Rae's gesture of caring and love brought tears to Janelle's eyes. Despite her young age and the trauma of her own loss, Rae's obvious empathy brought a surge of warmth and pride to Janelle. Her heart swelled with love for both of the girls.

Hailey tipped her head to meet Rae's. "I used to ask my mom if she could get me a little sister." Her voice had dropped to a tiny whisper. "I think she wanted to try, but then she got too sick."

Hailey's lower lipped trembled and so did Janelle's. It was all she could do not to cry. *Lord, please help this lonely child.*

Wanting to lighten the mood, she cleared her throat of the emotion of the moment as best she could.

"Tell you what, girls." She added a dose of enthusiasm to her words. "When we finish lunch, why don't we gather some pinecones and see if we can find some pretty wildflowers? When we get home, we can dry the flowers and make a wreath of them."

Hailey lifted her head, a puzzled look in her eyes. "I don't know how to dry flowers."

"Then I guess I'll have to teach you." Smiling, Janelle aimed a tickle finger at Hailey's tummy.

Giggling, she backed away and the somber clouds in her eyes vanished, leaving them sparkling and filled with youthful vitality.

After lunch they gathered a blanket full of pinecones, pine needles and a variety of grasses and wildflowers that hadn't yet turned to seed.

By the time Adam came into the house for dinner, Janelle and the girls had spread what they'd collected out on the kitchen table.

He stopped abruptly and pretended to scowl at the sight. "If you three were trying your hand at hunting and gathering for our dinner, you've got way too much fiber and not enough meat."

Janelle sputtered a laugh. "I suppose some of the wildflowers might be edible, but we have something else in mind."

"This isn't dinner, Daddy. We're going to make a wreath," Hailey announced.

Adam expelled an exaggerated sigh. "I'm sure glad to hear that. Now the question is, why?"

"Why not?" Janelle twisted a length of floss around the flower stems and tied a knot so she could hang them in a dark place for a few days.

"An autumn wreath will look nice on the front door. If I can find a few small crab apples, I'll add those to the wreath, too."

He gazed at her with thoughtful gray eyes in a way that brought a flush to her cheeks. He briefly shifted his attention to the collection on the table, then back to her. His lips hitched into a half smile.

"Guess fall will be here pretty soon, won't it?"

She swallowed hard. She hadn't meant to imply she'd still be living in his guest cottage when fall turned the aspen leaves yellow in the high country. Nor did she have a right to make plans that included him and his house so many weeks in the future.

Creating a stable home for Raeanne came first. A home of their own.

Breaking eye contact, she picked up another bunch of flowers. She could leave the wreath for Adam and Hailey to enjoy.

Or she could take it to the house she'd buy and hang it where she could remember the days she'd spent here with Adam and his daughter.

The memorable days of her first summer in Bear Lake.

Chapter Six

While Janelle checked her email on her laptop and dressed for a morning of house hunting, Rae-anne played with the kitten. Rae then carefully carried Kitty Cat to the main house, where she'd spend the day getting into mischief followed by a long nap.

More often than not, Rae's beloved Ruff was ignored except at bedtime. A healthy change, Janelle thought. Each day her little girl discarded more of the fears and insecurities that had struck her mute.

Dressed in a T-shirt and jeans, Adam was eating his breakfast at the kitchen table. "Where are you looking for houses today?"

Janelle plucked an English muffin from the toaster. "Sharon wants me to look at a couple of places in the upper lake area."

He spooned some cereal into his mouth. "Some

of the houses there are pretty isolated, and they get snow earlier in the winter than the lower lake does."

Sitting down across from him, Janelle sipped her coffee. "Is that bad?"

"It makes it harder to get out onto the highway if you're going anywhere early in the day after a snowfall. You'd need a four-wheel-drive vehicle for sure."

"Oh." She frowned. "How much snowfall do you get?"

"Maybe fifty inches total, spread out from October through April. It's not too bad. The lake actually moderates our weather compared to some places in Montana."

Maybe fifty inches of snow was not much for him, but she was from Seattle, where the customary precipitation came in the form of rain and drizzle, not snow. "The houses seemed a little less expensive there than closer to town."

He tossed back the last of his coffee and stood. "There's a reason for that. Not many year-round residents want to put up with the inconvenience."

"I suppose not." The photo and description of one house made it seem particularly attractive: three bedrooms on a half acre of land. But Janelle didn't relish the idea of being snowed in frequently with no close neighbors to offer help if she needed it. And what about getting Raeanne to school? Would winter weather pose a serious problem?

Rinsing his dishes, he put them in the dishwasher. "Say, the Pine Tree Diner has a Thursday night special, chicken and dumplings. How 'bout I take you and the girls out tonight?"

Startled by the invitation but pleased, Janelle said, "That sounds wonderful."

"Great. I'll see you this afternoon."

"You're sure it's all right to leave Rae here? I don't want her to become a pest."

"She and Hailey are fine together. When they get too bored, I'll put them to work changing oil or putting air in tires."

A quick frown pulled at Janelle's brow. "You will?"

"Hailey's getting pretty good at it." He winked and walked toward the door, leaving Janelle to wonder if he'd been kidding and why a simple wink would make her stomach flutter and her heart skip a beat.

"Don't worry," he called as he opened the door. "Hailey knows to stay close, where I can keep an eye on her."

She felt a measure of relief about Rae's safety, which did little to ease her feminine reaction to Adam.

Janelle returned from house hunting by lunchtime and found a white-haired woman pushing a vacuum down the hallway. The girls weren't anywhere in sight.

"Hello," she called, but apparently the woman couldn't hear her. She called louder just as the woman turned off the vacuum.

The woman whirled and screamed.

"I'm so sorry. I didn't mean to frighten you."

"Land's sake, you did give me a fright." Her pale white cheeks had turned red, and she patted her chest as though catching her breath. "You must be that Mrs. Townsend that Adam mentioned. Said you and your little girl were living here for a bit."

"In the cottage," Janelle quickly clarified. "Adam was kind enough to let me and my daughter stay there while we're hunting for a house of our own."

"Well, isn't that sweet of him. I'm Mrs. Murphy. Been cleaning the house and taking care of Adam and his girl ever since his dear wife got so sick. I think it's purely nice that he's got a new woman in his life. Lisa was a dear girl, but she's been gone awhile now. Time he moved on. Yes, sirree, that's what I think."

"No, it's not like. I'm not in his life. At least not that way. I am helping him out with—"

Her explanation came too late. The woman had turned her vacuum back on and had moved into Hailey's bedroom.

Janelle exhaled. She'd really like to correct Mrs. Murphy's impression, but it seemed useless to try. She'd believe what she wanted. No amount of protest would change her mind.

She found the girls outside and asked them to come in for lunch. She made them and herself sandwiches, then carried an additional sandwich and a glass of milk out to the garage for Adam.

"Hey, thanks." He wiped his hands on a cloth. "I'd forgotten all about lunch. Let me wash up a bit."

Janelle had already realized he often skipped lunch, which meant he was a big eater at dinner. Idly she wondered if his late wife used to bring him lunch. If nothing else, they could have spent a few minutes together during the day. Janelle would have thought that a treat with Raymond, but he hadn't wanted the interruption to his work.

A sharp pang of regret, or perhaps it was anger, caught her in the midsection.

Since she had taken the chair at Adam's desk in order to get some work done, he sat in the straight-back guest chair to eat.

"I met your housekeeper, Mrs. Murphy. She seems to have the wrong impression about me."

His brows rose. "Oh?"

"She seemed to think… She has this misunderstanding that you and I—"

He was quick to wave off her concerns. "Don't worry about Mrs. Murphy. She'll figure it out eventually."

Janelle hoped that would be sooner rather than later. She didn't want either she or Adam to be the subject of rumors around town.

"So how did the house hunting go?" He took a big bite of his roast-beef sandwich.

"You were right. Sharon confirmed the road along the upper lake was among the last to be plowed, and neighbors—particularly year-round neighbors—are pretty far apart."

"So that's a no go, right?"

"I asked to look at places a little closer to town."

With his mouth full, he nodded and appeared pleased with her decision.

She picked up a two-year-old invoice she'd been working on. "I don't recognize this vendor and can't tell what you purchased." She handed him the invoice, which he placed on the desk without looking at it.

"What does it say?" He made a show of examining his sandwich, checking to see that the lettuce was in place.

She pointed at the letterhead. "It's from Global Supply. The amount is over a thousand dollars, but the product description is gibberish to me."

"Oh, that was a part for one of my hydraulic lifts that broke."

She made a note on the invoice. "Is it something I should depreciate or take as an expense?"

He stopped chewing and stared at her blankly. "I don't know. What's the difference?"

No wonder he'd had trouble filing his tax returns. In addition to not understanding depreciation, he'd put invoices and customer billings all in the same file folder, sometimes not even marking if they were paid. She'd had to cross-check with his bank statements to confirm one way or the other.

She briefly explained depreciation and how it worked. "But since you didn't carry forward any depreciation, I think I should take it as an expense. It will be less confusing to the IRS."

"I'm all for that."

"By the way, you may have noticed I've put together a more cohesive filing system." She opened the drawer that she had formerly been unable to close due to so many papers crammed inside. "This year's invoices go in this first folder. You need to mark them paid and write the check number on them. I've done the same thing with last year's records and the year before. It'll be much easier to find things now."

"Whatever you want." Abruptly, he finished his sandwich and downed his milk, then wiped his mouth with the sleeve of his overalls. "That was great, but I'd better get back to work. I've got a sticky carburetor to fix."

He walked back to the car he'd been working on, and it struck Janelle as odd that he'd never looked at the Global Supply invoice to either confirm the amount or the part he'd purchased two years ago. Nor had he indicated any interest in the new filing system.

He either had the memory of an elephant or he was hiding the fact he needed glasses to read and didn't want to embarrass himself in front of her. Maybe both.

She smiled to herself. A man's ego could be so fragile.

Adam heaved a sigh of relief as he stuck his head under the hood of an aging four-door the owner had been keeping together with little more that chewing gum and chicken wire.

He'd almost blown his cover with Janelle. It was plain lucky he'd remembered the hydraulic part he'd bought from Global. If he'd had to read that invoice, his secret would have been obvious.

And her filing system? Yeah, sure, he could handle that—in his dreams.

He fought a wash of shame that sent a flush of heat up his neck. *Stupid!*

He wished she'd left his stuff alone. Forget that he'd asked her to help him with the taxes. Until she'd showed up, he'd known where everything was. Which pile was which. Sort of.

He twisted his wrench so hard he almost broke off the nut holding the carburetor in place. How dumb would that be, he chided himself. He'd nearly made a mess of this little job and turned the carburetor into a basket case he'd have to replace with his own money.

If he had any left when the IRS finished with him.

Maybe he shouldn't have hired Janelle to redo his tax filings. She could have stayed here anyway while she was house hunting. They could spend evenings out on the boat, maybe have a dinner picnic in a quiet bay he knew across the lake.

That way she wouldn't have a reason to ask him to read something. Wouldn't *organize* his life for him. He wouldn't risk revealing his shortcomings. She'd see him as a successful mechanic and garage owner.

Until the IRS locked him behind bars.

That evening, with Janelle beside him and the girls in the small backseat, Adam pulled his pickup into the crowded parking lot in front of the Pine Tree Diner. The three-story restaurant, which was painted a bright pink with white trim, always drew a crowd. The sign out front announced they served breakfast, lunch and dinner. Homemade pies and authentic Czech dishes were their specialties.

Although it wasn't on the lake side of Main Street and didn't have a view, it was still a popular spot for locals looking for a cup of coffee and conversation or a good, filling meal.

"Hey, Adam." Alisa Machak, a blonde with her hair tied back in a ponytail, came out from behind the cash register to greet them. Several years younger than Adam, she gave Janelle and the girls a quick once-over.

Adam made introductions, adding, "Janelle's looking to buy a house around here."

"That's great. You'll like living in Bear Lake." Alisa grabbed some menus for them. "Table for four?"

"Hope you have one available," Adam said. "Looks like you're pretty busy." The pink upholstered booths and the counter seats were all filled, the room noisy with conversation.

"We always are for Thursday night specials. Come on back with me."

"How's your son doing?" Adam asked.

She glanced over her shoulder. "Greg's fine. But *I'm* ready for school to start. So's Mama."

Adam laughed. "I hear you on that."

They followed her into a room filled with tables, most of which were occupied. On Friday and Saturday nights the diner had live music performed on a small stage at one end of the room. An open door led out to a patio eating area with tables shaded by large pink umbrellas.

"Inside or out?" she asked.

"Is it warm enough to eat outside?" Janelle asked. "Seems like the evenings have started to cool off."

"If you get cold, we've got overhead heaters. We can turn one on."

Janelle checked with Adam.

"Let's do outside," he said.

Sitting down, Janelle was amused at how Hailey arranged to sit next to Raeanne, which left Janelle and Adam sitting next to each other. She was being quite the little mother. Or was she playing matchmaker?

Janelle frowned at the thought. She didn't mind Hailey "mothering" Raeanne, although she felt Hailey should be spending more time with her own friends.

As for the matchmaking? That wasn't going to happen. Not anytime soon. She'd made a mistake when she'd married Raymond. She wasn't eager to leap into another relationship, not when her judgment had been so poor the first time.

Alisa placed menus in front of Janelle and Adam and gave children's menus to both girls.

"What can I bring you to drink?" she asked.

Janelle looked up. "I'll have iced tea and Rae-anne will have milk."

"Ditto for us," Adam said.

"Dad, are you going to get your favorite buffalo burger tonight?" Hailey asked.

"Not tonight, squirt. I'm going with the special. Buffalo burgers are best at lunchtime."

Alisa said, "I'll bring your drinks and some bread while you have a chance to study the menu and decide what you'd like to have for dinner."

As Janelle read through the menu, she noted several traditional Czechoslovakian offerings, including potato pancakes. She decided she'd try the chicken and dumplings tonight and come back another time to try other specialties of the house.

"How does it happen they have so many Czech items on the menu?" she asked Adam.

"Mama and Papa Machak moved over from Czechoslovakia and bought the diner before I was born. They live in the top two floors and used to rent rooms until they bought the motel next door, the Pine Tree Inn. Pop Machak died several years ago and left Mama Machak and her daughter, Alisa, to run the place."

"Looks like they're doing a good job. They're certainly busy enough."

"It slows down after the tourist season, but the locals keep coming."

Keeping a restaurant profitable was no easy

trick. At this point, the Pine Tree Diner appeared to be thriving.

Janelle asked Rae, "What do you want to eat, sweetie?"

Rae puzzled over her menu. Although she could actually read a few basic words, the menu exceeded her prekindergarten skill level.

"Hey, Peanut, why don't you tell Rae what's on the menu?" Adam suggested.

Glancing toward her father, Hailey said, "Sure." She proceeded to read down the list of items.

For a moment, Janelle wondered why Adam had made a point of asking Hailey to read the menu for Rae, since it would have been just as easy for him to help her. She shrugged off the thought as unimportant, deciding to enjoy the view instead of worrying about it.

The sky above the forested hillside to the west was beginning to show the first hints of color as the sun began its descent over the horizon. How nice it would be, since it was unlikely she could afford lakefront property, to have a porch to sit on to watch the sun set at the end of each day. She'd have to put that on her wish list of house amenities.

Not only was Montana big-sky country, but it also was God's country, and she thanked the Lord for leading her here.

She glanced at Adam next to her and found him gazing at her, the hint of a smile teasing the corners of his lips. Their arms all but touching, a warm sense of pleasure, of being in the right place, brought a matching smile to her lips.

Had the Lord brought her not only to Montana but to Adam, as well?

It was far too early to jump to that conclusion. They'd known each other only a week. Not nearly long enough to be considering any kind of a relationship except friendship.

When she'd discovered Raymond's infidelities, she'd vowed to heal herself and achieve stability for Rae before she even considered having another man in her life.

Whatever might be possible between her and Adam would simply have to wait. Maybe forever.

That thought brought a sting of regret, which she immediately tamped down.

As they strolled back to the car after dinner, Hailey and Raeanne each took one of Janelle's hands. A cute gesture on Hailey's part, which Janelle suspected was linked to the girl still missing her own mother.

Janelle would have to be careful not to get too close to Hailey, as much as that seemed hard to avoid with such an outgoing, naturally loving child. But she didn't want Hailey hurt when she and Rae found their own place and moved out.

Adam had stopped to speak to a friend in the

parking lot. It occurred to Janelle that this was a good time to ask Hailey a question that had been bothering her all day.

"Hailey, does you dad wear glasses?"

The girl stopped abruptly. A crease formed between her eyebrows. "No, he doesn't need glasses."

"I just wondered. This afternoon, it almost seemed like—"

"I'm going to go tell Dad to come on or he'll talk to that guy forever." She slipped her hand from Janelle's and dashed back through the parking lot toward her father.

"We'll meet you at the truck," Janelle called after her, thinking Hailey's reaction to her question wasn't at all what she had expected. It was almost as if she knew a secret about Adam that she didn't want to share.

A secret that had nothing to do with glasses.

Chapter Seven

Janelle got her car back on Saturday, all shiny-new looking.

Impulsively, she threw her arms around Adam's neck and hugged him. "Thank you! Thank you! It looks beautiful."

For a moment, Adam tensed, but then let his arms slide around her waist. "You're welcome."

She caught the not-unpleasant scent of auto grease and oil along with a hint of his shampoo and felt the warmth and strength of his body pressed against hers. A tremor rippled through her. Of need? Or longing?

Stepping back, she was snared by his eyes. No longer gray, they'd gone nearly black.

She licked her lips. Cleared her throat.

"You'd better take your car for a spin." His voice had a rusty quality she didn't recognize. "See how it handles."

"Yes. Of course." But her feet didn't budge. As if someone had used superglue on the soles of her shoes, she couldn't seem to move.

"I'll get the key for you." He, too, seemed trapped by some unseen force.

"That would be good."

"The key's in my office."

"I know. For cars you're working on, you hang keys on a Peg-Board near the desk and lock the office at night so they'll be safe."

"I wouldn't want anyone to steal a customer's car."

"You're a very responsible man." Every time she spoke, her voice dipped lower and grew more breathy.

"I'll get your key," he repeated.

"Yes."

"Hey, boss!" Vern shouted. "You order new tires for McCloud's truck?"

Adam blinked as though coming out of a trance. So did Janelle.

"They're piled outside the door," he responded.

"I'll get 'em."

Adam visibly drew a deep breath. "I'll be right back with your key."

Unsure what, if anything, had just transpired between them, Janelle could only nod. Having her own car back was a good thing. She wouldn't have to borrow Adam's clunker. She'd be independent again, able to leave anytime she wanted to. She ignored the voice in her heart that reminded her that she didn't want to leave—not yet.

Almost reluctantly, she got into her car and drove out of the garage. The engine sounded as if it had been well oiled, the gears shifted smoothly. A job well done.

After a few minutes she returned to the garage. Adam was lying on his back under a car.

"My car runs beautifully," she said to his big feet, the only part of him she could see. "What do I owe you?"

"I put the bill on the desk." His voice was muffled by a couple tons of steel. "There's no rush."

"I'll go ahead and pay you. Then I'll send a copy to my insurance."

"Fine by me."

She cocked her head to one side. Five minutes ago they'd nearly...what? Apparently whatever they'd nearly done mattered little to Adam.

He hadn't even stuck his head out from under the car to look her in the eye.

Men! And they claimed women were hard to understand.

Sunday morning, Raeanne stood patiently in front of the mirror while Janelle braided two small sections of her hair, then pulled them to the back and held them with a pretty clip.

"My, don't you look fancy for church." Janelle kissed the top of her daughter's head. She loved fussing with Rae's hair, feeling the soft strands slip through her fingers. Combing her hair was right up there with hugs and kisses, a quiet mother-daughter moment that could be locked away in a memory box and retrieved later as needed.

Kitty Cat was far less serene about the whole hairdo thing. She kept batting at the comb on the dresser or mock fighting with the kitten in the mirror, which brought gales of giggles from Rae-anne—and equal joy to Janelle.

The sound of her daughter's voice was a gift, an answer to her prayers.

Ready for breakfast, Rae picked up the kitten and carried it to the main house. Janelle opened the sliding door.

"Good morning, all," she said.

Hailey hopped up from her chair at the kitchen table. "Rae, I love your hair! You look so cute."

"Would you like me to do your hair that way, too?" Janelle asked.

Hailey brightened. "Oh, wow! Could you?"

"Of course. Bring me your comb and brush and a clip you like. And a mirror, too."

She raced off toward her room with Raeanne in her wake followed by a bounding Kitty Cat.

Janelle strolled toward the kitchen, where Adam sat at the table eating his breakfast.

"Looks like we haven't yet plumbed the depths of your domestic talents." He got up to pour her a cup of coffee.

"Blame it on a misspent childhood styling dolls' hair. Which, by the way, eventually meant I had a whole closet full of bald dolls."

He nearly dropped the coffeepot and laughed. "I don't think Hailey would look real good bald, if you don't mind."

"Not to worry." She grinned and sipped the rich coffee he'd managed to pour into her mug. "My technique has improved considerably since I've had Raeanne as my subject."

The girls came running back, Hailey with brush and comb in hand.

"Rae, sweetie, show Adam what you want for breakfast while I fix Hailey's hair." She took Hailey by the shoulders, turned her around and had her sit on the floor in front of her. She ran a brush through the girl's long, blond hair. "Your hair's very fine. It might be easier to manage if you cut it shorter, right about to here."

Rae hopped up in the chair next to Janelle with the bowl of cereal Adam had poured for her.

Hailey studied herself in the mirror. "I don't know. I'm used to it long."

"That's all right. Let me make you a couple of braids, and we'll see how that looks."

Busying herself making the braids, Janelle noticed Adam studying what she was doing. "It's not hard. You just twist three strands of hair together and pin them in place."

"I remember at camp one summer when I was a kid making a leather belt that way. After about a week, the whole belt fell apart."

"The good thing about hair is that you can brush it out and start all over. No harm done."

He didn't look convinced.

When Janelle finished the braids and clipped them in place, Hailey looked in the mirror. "That is so cool!" Standing, she threw herself into Janelle's arms. "Thank you so much. I love the braids!"

"You're more than welcome." She hugged Hailey back. "Now, I'd better eat some breakfast or all through the church service my stomach will be growling as loud as a cow with a bellyache."

Hailey giggled.

An hour later, as they were walking into church, Hailey opted to go to Sunday school to see her friends.

As she ran off toward the classrooms, Adam said, "That was very nice of you to fix her hair like that. It looks good."

"It was easy and fun to do."

"Yeah, maybe. Lisa used to curl her hair and stuff." He shrugged, although Janelle thought he was acting more casual about his late wife that he actually felt. "I don't have the knack. I turn into all thumbs. Guess she'll have to learn how to do it on her own."

Or maybe someday he'd fall in love and marry another woman, Janelle mused. A woman who loved to fuss with a child's hair.

A lump formed in her throat as she realized that the woman was unlikely to be her. He deserved someone who wasn't carrying the burden of a marriage that had been a sham.

After church, Adam climbed into his truck. The girls squeezed into the fold-down seats of the extended cab, and Janelle took the passenger seat.

This morning when Janelle had fixed Hailey's hair, he'd suddenly realized how fast his little girl was growing up. While he had a couple of years until she reached the teenage years, she was well on her way. Soon he wouldn't dare call her Peanut or squirt. She'd be too big. Too grown-up for silly nicknames and hanging around her old man.

Where had the time gone?

Janelle snapped her seat belt in place. "If you're in no rush, could we drive by a house Sharon showed me yesterday? It's not far, and I'd appreciate you taking a look. See what you think, if any big problems pop out at you."

"Sure. Tell me where."

She gave him directions. "It's not very big, only two bedrooms. But there's a basement and the kitchen has been remodeled recently. Sharon said it was only a block to the school bus stop."

Adam took a left out of the parking lot. His heart clutched at the thought of Janelle actually finding a house she liked. He was getting used to her being around. Eating breakfast across the table from her. Sitting on the deck together watching the stars come out.

Even watching her create a fancy hairdo for Hailey. Something he didn't have a clue how to do.

Just like he couldn't keep a handle on the paperwork for the garage. And now that she'd rearranged everything, put it all in neat and tidy files, he couldn't even find what he wanted without asking her to dig it out for him.

And wouldn't you know, she'd started rearranging the cupboards in the kitchen, too. It had taken him forever to find the peanut butter yesterday. Apparently she'd bought some natural peanut-butter brand that was supposed to be healthier and required refrigeration.

How was he supposed to know that? It was okay, he supposed, but didn't taste like the old stuff.

She was bringing a lot of changes into his house. Into his life. Although most of them he liked.

Others just plain made him nervous. Like the way she kept sticking invoices or bills under his nose expecting him to tell her what they were about.

"There it is, on the right." She pointed at a small

ranch-style house with white stucco and green trim. The lot was fairly big and backed onto a forested area. "The house is vacant, so you can park in the driveway. You can see the mountains from the porch, a great place to watch sunsets."

They all climbed out of the truck. The girls raced up onto the porch and tried to peer through the windows.

Adam walked alongside the house, taking a look at the roof, which seemed solid. There was an obvious dip in the backyard that was bound to turn into a lake when it rained.

"I thought it was nice to have some forested area behind the house," Janelle said.

"Maybe not so much in this case." He walked into the woods a few feet and stopped. Did she really want to buy this place? She ought to have something bigger. More elegant, to match her style.

"What's wrong?"

"See those snow markers with the red tips?"

"Is that what they are?"

"Yep. This is a snowmobile route." He motioned for her to step out into what was a wide trail between the trees. "This runs from town up through the national forest area and comes back out to the highway at Summers. During the winter this turns into a freeway, with those noisy snowmobiles roaring up and down, scaring the wildlife to death and the drivers risking their own lives and limbs in the process."

Janelle's forehead puckered and she pursed her lips. "It's pretty close to the house, isn't it?"

"Closer than I'd like."

She hooked her hand behind her neck and rubbed. "Sharon didn't mention this."

He shrugged. "Maybe she's not familiar with the trail."

"Maybe."

In the distance, he heard the low rumble of approaching vehicles. "Let's step back into the trees. We're about to have company." Taking her elbow, he led her off the trail.

Within minutes, three all-terrain vehicles roared by, making enough noise to break a few eardrums.

When they passed, Adam said, "I forgot to mention that ATVs use this trail the rest of the year."

"Swell." Shoulders slumped, she turned to walk back to the house.

He caught up with her. "I'm sorry. I know you thought this one was a real possibility."

"It would pretty much be a bad idea to buy a place in a nice, quiet neighborhood only to find out you're living in the middle of a speedway where amateurs think they're driving the Indianapolis 500."

"It's worse on weekends than during the week. Maybe you and Rae could set up a hot-chocolate stand next to the trail. Make yourselves a bunch of money."

She whacked his arm with the back of her hand, but the hint of a smile softened the blow. "Thanks for the suggestion, but I think I'll keep looking."

"Good idea." Satisfied that he'd successfully delayed the day she'd move out of his cottage for at least a little while, he hooked his thumbs in the pockets of his jeans and strolled back to the truck.

As the week progressed, Janelle became more and more anxious about the IRS hearing on Friday. She'd checked her numbers a dozen times. But would that be enough? What if she'd made a mistake?

As soon as Adam returned from his weekly Rotary luncheon, she corralled him in the garage.

"Adam, I really need to talk to you about the hearing Friday."

"You've squared all the paperwork away, haven't you?"

"Yes. In fact, based on your revised tax returns, you'll probably owe some penalties but overall much less than what the IRS is claiming."

"That's a relief." He dragged his overalls off of a hanger and tugged them on over his jeans.

"I need to explain to you how I arrived at the bottom line so you can answer questions if anything comes up."

He stopped pulling up the overall zipper and gaped at her. His ruddy complexion paled. "You're going to be there, aren't you? You're coming with me, right?"

"Yes, I'll come along. But I need to brief you so you'll understand and can answer the questions yourself."

He shook his head. "No need if you're there." He started to walk away.

"Yes, there is!" She raised her voice. "What if I've made a mistake? What if I misinterpreted something? I'm not a tax expert or a CPA. You're the one who's going to pay for my errors."

"Janie, I have complete faith in your work. You don't make mistakes."

Janie? Her jaw dropped open. No one except her mother had ever called her Janie.

She snapped her mouth closed. Opened it again. "You at least have to sign the forms. It's the law. The IRS won't accept them without your signature."

He lifted his shoulders in an easy shrug. "No problem. Show me where I need to sign."

She marked the lines where he needed to sign with a red X and watched him while he scribbled something that vaguely resembled a signature.

Why had he called her Janie? Had he simply blurted it out because he was too lazy to say

"Janelle"? Or could using her nickname be a sign of affection?

And did she really want to know the answer to either of those questions?

Chapter Eight

The ride to the IRS office in Missoula wound through a scenic forest before reaching a lower elevation and rolling hillsides covered with a carpet of summer-brown grass.

They had dropped the girls off at Mrs. Murphy's house. Although not thrilled with the prospect, they took all sorts of games to keep themselves occupied.

"Are you nervous about the hearing?" Sitting in the passenger seat of Adam's truck, Janelle held tightly to her briefcase. Dressed in a rust-colored suit that she thought of as her interview outfit, she knew she looked professional. But that didn't alleviate her anxiety. What if she made some horrible mistake that would sink Adam's business?

"Mostly I just want them to take the lien off my bank accounts so I can get back to business as usual." Adam had dressed up, too, wearing a

Western-cut blue shirt with a string tie. He looked more like a handsome cowboy out on the town than a garage mechanic.

"When we reach an agreement about how much you owe and set up a payment plan, the agent should be willing to do that." *If* her computations were right.

Adam puffed his cheeks and blew out a sigh. "At the government's usual speed, I'll be an old man before the paperwork gets through the system and the bank's notified."

"I'm a little more optimistic than that." She hoped they could persuade the agent to act quickly.

Once they entered the town, traffic increased. Janelle found herself gaping at all the cars and shops and buildings more than six stories tall, as if she'd never been to a big city. Which was funny, since Missoula didn't compare to the metropolitan area of Seattle, where she'd lived most of her life.

She laughed at herself. Bear Lake and its quiet beauty had spoiled her for anything else.

They didn't have to wait long in the lobby before Agent Fred Hart called them into his office. Probably in his late thirties, he was coatless with his sleeves rolled up and his tie loose at his collar.

Adam introduced himself and Janelle, and they exchanged handshakes.

"Now then…" Hart sat behind his desk and dragged a file off the pile next to him. "I know most folks are terrorized when they hear *IRS hearing,* but I promise you I'm not here to nail you with big fines or anything like that. Our job at the IRS is to see that everyone pays what they rightfully owe and no more than that."

"Glad to hear it." Crossing his legs, Adam rested one hand on his knee, looking casual and at ease.

"Ms. Townsend, are you representing Mr. Hunter as his CPA?"

"No, sir, I'm not a CPA. But I have acted as his bookkeeper. I prepared his revised tax forms." She pulled the two files from her briefcase and handed them to Hart. "I think you'll find he owes considerably less, including penalties, than the IRS had assessed."

"Hmm." He flipped through the pages, scanning quickly, then went to the original copy of Adam's returns. He looked directly at Adam. "You've got some big discrepancies between these two returns. Care to explain that?"

"I messed up. Janelle redid everything. She can probably explain the changes better than I can."

Annoyed that Adam hadn't let her show him what she'd done so he could discuss the returns himself, she proceeded to defend the changes in both income and expenses. She indicated she had backup material for each of her entries with her if he cared to check them.

"I believe Mr. Hunter made a series of honest

mistakes," she said when she concluded her explanation. "He did pay what he thought he owed, so it's obvious he wasn't trying to dodge his responsibilities. And as it turned out, the amount he paid for both years is quite close to the actual amount he owed when recalculated."

Hart raised his brows and shifted his attention back to Adam. "So you are the one who completed these initial forms?"

Lowering his leg, Adam started tapping his foot. He folded his arms across his chest. "I admit I made a lot of mistakes."

"If you aren't capable of completing your tax returns, why didn't you hire someone like Ms. Townsend to do them for you initially?"

"I'm capable." A muscle flexed in his jaw. "I was busy. Careless. There's no law against that."

"Actually, there is." The agent turned to the computer beside his desk, brought up a file and began to enter data.

Janelle tried to read the numbers on the screen, but the angle was all wrong for her to be able to see them clearly. Nerves twisted in her stomach. What if she'd made a ton of mistakes, too? Would Hart come up with a number that Adam couldn't afford to pay? What if he had to mortgage the garage and house?

Her mouth went dry. "I'm sure if Mr. Hunter owes a substantial amount he can work out a payment plan. His garage is a successful business, and he's well respected in the community."

Hart swiveled back to face them. "Because of your underpayment and penalties, you're looking at a chunk of money." He named an amount that was quite reasonable.

Relief drained the tension from Janelle's shoulders.

Adam leaned forward and braced his hands on the edge of the desk. "Is that all?"

"You'll receive an official document within thirty days and will have another thirty days to make the payment."

"Wow! That's great." A full-blown grin creased Adam's cheek.

"Will you be able to release the lien on his bank accounts soon? It's difficult to run a business without access to a line of credit," Janelle pointed out. "And if he owes such a relatively small amount—"

"I'll take care of that," Hart promised. "It will take a few days to make it through the system, but by the end of next week you'll have access to your accounts again."

"Thank you." Adam started to stand.

"I have some advice for you, Mr. Hunter. Don't ever try to complete an IRS form again. Ms. Townsend has saved your bacon this time. I suggest you continue to employ her—and give her a raise."

"Yes, sir! I think I can promise that."

After another round of handshakes, Adam and Janelle left the agent's office. They made it as far as the middle of the lobby when Adam pulled her toward him. He framed her face with his strong, gentle hands.

"Janie, you are the greatest!"

He lowered his mouth over hers, warm and firm and somehow shocking. The kiss took her breath away. Her heart soared.

When he broke the kiss, he smiled as though he'd conquered Mount Everest. *All because of a favorable tax hearing?*

Meanwhile, her heart was doing a mambo that had nothing to do with the IRS.

A ripple of applause from those waiting in the lobby shattered the moment.

Janelle groaned. Or maybe it was a moan. Her cheeks flamed. She'd never expected to make a public spectacle of herself, but she couldn't regret the moment. The kiss. Anyway, it was Adam who had made them the center of attention, and he didn't appear the least contrite. Quite the opposite. He looked as dazed by the kiss as she felt.

He grabbed her arm. "Let's get out of here."

Adam helped Janelle into the truck. How had that kiss happened? He wasn't usually so impulsive. But there he was, and there she was, and if truth be told he'd been thinking a lot lately about kissing her.

Not a real smart idea, guitar boy.

Maybe not. But he'd liked it a lot. Probably more than he should.

No doubt a sophisticated big-city woman like Janelle wouldn't appreciate being kissed in a room full of strangers. She deserved soft lights, music playing in the background, a smooth guy who knew the right words to say.

Instead he'd laid one on her like an overeager adolescent who couldn't wait to get her alone.

He walked around to the driver's door and yanked it open. He jammed the key in the ignition.

"Look, about that kiss." He turned in the seat to look at her. Her face still carried the rosy glow of her blush. He'd embarrassed her. "I hope you aren't angry."

Her brown eyes widened. "Why would I be angry?"

A matching flush crept up his neck. "Because you deserve better than a big ole smooch in front of half the world."

One corner of her lips lifted. "I take it you mean that as a compliment."

"Well, yeah, but I was out of line. I shouldn't have embarrassed you. I'm sorry." Lisa had hated to make a scene in public. Janelle had probably been mortified to be kissed in front of strangers.

She fastened her seat belt and faced forward, that little smile still teasing her lips. "I'm not sorry at all."

He stared at her profile. A nice straight nose. Lips that were quick to smile and delicious to kiss. A chin that hinted at a stubborn streak. All of the pieces went together as if they'd been created by a fine portrait artist.

She wasn't embarrassed by his kiss?

Oh, boy! Was he ever in trouble!

Straightening, with a shaking hand, he twisted the key in the ignition. "Let's see if we can find someplace to eat. I'm starved."

A block away he found a family restaurant. The hostess led them to a booth and gave them menus. He sat on the opposite side from Janelle. No way was he going to slide around to sit close to her. He'd already made enough of a mess for one day.

She isn't mad, a small voice in his head reminded him. Didn't matter. He'd stepped over a line he hadn't intended to cross. *Yeah, but you liked it. A lot.*

He opened the menu and scanned the pictures along the side. A hamburger and fries were always safe to order.

A waiter, who looked to be in his seventies and aging fast, brought them water and was ready to take their orders.

"I'll have the chicken-walnut salad with Gorgonzola," Janelle said. "And a diet soda."

Adam pointed to a picture on the menu. "Hamburger—cooked medium-rare, please—and fries for me."

"You aren't going to have their specialty?" Her voice rose in surprise.

He frowned. "What specialty?"

The waiter started to answer but Janelle beat him to it. "It says all over the menu that they have the best buffalo burgers in Montana. I thought you'd want to compare them to the ones at the Pine Tree Diner that you like so much."

Despite the fact that he really liked buffalo burgers and would have ordered one if he'd known it was on the menu, he hedged to disguise his secret weakness. "Maybe next time. Besides, the diner's buffalo burgers are hard to beat. I'll go with the regular burger for now. And a regular soda."

The waiter seemed satisfied with their orders and walked away.

Janelle was frowning at him.

Leaning back, he tried for casual. "Something the matter?"

"No. But I am curious."

He knew what was coming. He didn't want to have this conversation. Not with Janelle or anybody else.

"You know what they say about curiosity and

the cat." He unwrapped the pieces of silverware from the paper napkin and put them in their proper place.

"I've never seen you read anything."

"So?" He reached for the soda the waiter had delivered and downed a big swallow. He almost choked on it. "I'm not much for reading. Guys are all about action, you know?"

Her gaze never left him. "Most guys can read a menu."

"What makes you think I can't read a menu?" He added all the offense he could muster to his retort. "I ordered a burger and fries, didn't I? It was there on the menu, wasn't it?"

She reached across the table and touched his hand, her fingers warm against the cold that had seeped into him. "You didn't know they had buffalo burgers on the menu." It wasn't a question but rather a statement of fact. "The picture looked just like a regular burger."

He yanked his hand back. "That doesn't mean anything."

"At first I thought you needed glasses and were too macho to wear them. But then I realized you do some pretty close work on engines and whatever else there is under the hood of a car. So I began to think maybe there was something else the matter."

He ground his teeth together. "There's nothing the matter with me. Back off, okay?"

"I have a college friend who is absolutely brilliant. Close to being a genius. In four years she earned two degrees. One in ornithology and one in business management. She is also dyslexic."

"Yeah, but some of us aren't even close to being geniuses." He slapped the palm of his hand on the table, making her flinch and pull her hand away. He hated himself for frightening her. But he couldn't talk about it. The fact that he was too stupid to read a menu. The fact that he'd been hiding his problem all of his life. Adapting and faking it since as early as he could remember.

But Janelle Townsend was too perceptive to be fooled. She'd found him out.

Now, as sure as 20/20 oil froze up an engine in the first cold snap of winter, she'd freeze him out of her life.

Dear Lord, I never should have kissed her, because now I'll never be able to forget her.

Chapter Nine

Janelle hated his silence.

He wasn't going to talk to her.

He hadn't said a word while they ate their lunch. When they'd finished, he'd paid the check and they'd gone back to the truck.

Her heart ached for him. She hadn't meant to hurt him. Instead, she wanted to help him. But she'd learned from her college friend Eileen that until a person with dyslexia admits he has a problem and asks for help, it was no use to nag him. It didn't matter how much his refusal to address his handicap limited his life and made him self-conscious. Even defensive.

What a waste of a good man.

Yet look how much he'd accomplished in his life despite his limitations. He owned a successful business, was raising a beautiful daughter, was active in his church and the community.

How hardheaded he must be to keep his problem a secret rather than seek help.

"You know it's not your fault," she said.

He remained stoically silent, his focus on the road.

"Being dyslexic is nothing to be ashamed of."

He shot her a bruising look. "What do you know about being ashamed? How many times have you been called stupid? Laughed at because you couldn't read the simplest sentence in a first-grade book? Bullied every day by guys who weren't worth spit? Tell me that, Janelle. How many times have you hated yourself for being as dumb as an ox?"

"You're not dumb."

He snorted. "No, I'm not. But all through grade school that's the message I got from other kids and most of the teachers."

Anger flared at those thoughtless children and the adults who had let Adam suffer. "Didn't anyone try to help you?"

He took a turn a little too fast, and the truck tires squealed.

Janelle grabbed for the armrest as he let up on the accelerator.

"My parents tried to help. They talked to the principal. My teachers. But it didn't do much good."

"Shame on them!" She bit out the words.

"Weren't there any reading specialists who could help you?"

"Bear Lake isn't the big city. In those days, the school district didn't have money for specialists or any extra frills. We had to raise money for our football uniforms and travel expenses to get to games."

That gave Janelle a bad feeling. Before she settled permanently in Bear Lake, she'd better check out the schools. She wouldn't want Raeanne to receive less than the best education possible.

"By the time I reached high school," he continued, "I was big enough and tough enough to take care of myself. And I'd become a master at faking it. I might have graduated with all D's, but the teachers loved me." He said that with a laugh that didn't ring true.

"It's criminal that no one gave you any real help. There's no telling what you could have become. What you could have accomplished." Not that he hadn't become a wonderful mechanic. But if he'd gotten the help he'd needed, he could have become an engineer and designed the cars he worked on.

"I'm fine right where I am. I've got a good life. There's nothing else I'd want to be or do."

No other dreams? That might be the saddest thing she'd ever heard.

For a time, Janelle sat in silence, watching the

passing cars and listening to the hum of the tires on the highway.

"My friend Eileen told me there is all sorts of help online. Study aids. Exercises."

"Don't you get it?" He shook his head. "I don't want or need any help."

He'd certainly needed help completing his tax forms.

"Did your wife know you're dyslexic?" she asked softly.

"Yeah. I couldn't keep that from her. She needed to know."

Which was why she'd handled the paperwork for the garage. "What about Hailey? Does she know?"

He squeezed the steering wheel so hard his knuckles turned white. "No. My wife didn't want her to know, and you're not going to tell her. I don't want her to be ashamed of her old man. We're fine just as we are."

Janelle gasped. His wife didn't want— "You can't keep a secret like that from your daughter."

"I can and I will!" Like an angry grizzly bear, he all but bared his teeth at her and growled. "Don't even think of sticking your nose into my business."

Pressing her lips together, she looked out the window again at the passing scenery. When Janelle had asked Hailey about Adam needing glasses, the girl had run off. She hadn't wanted to discuss the subject. *Because she already knew her father's secret?*

She glanced back to Adam, studied the determined jut of his chin, the hard line of his lips.

"You know if you keep a secret like that from your daughter, you're teaching her to keep secrets from you."

"That's nonsense," he said without a moment's thought. "Hailey is the most honest person I know. We're tight, you know what I mean? She'd never keep a secret from me."

"Maybe she hasn't kept anything from you so far. But that doesn't mean somewhere down the line she'll tell you the whole truth about every single thing in her life. Not if you've taught her keeping secrets is okay. You have to tell her, Adam."

"No." He turned on the radio and raised the volume, effectively ending the conversation.

Hurt, and worried he'd be in for a shock one day when his daughter didn't meet his expectations, Janelle turned away. If he didn't want and wouldn't accept her help, there was nothing she could do except pray that God would intervene.

A good man like Adam could use the Lord's helping hand. He sure hadn't gotten the help he'd needed from his teachers or the school district.

They stopped at Mrs. Murphy's house to pick up the girls.

Hailey let Rae climb into the back first and then followed her.

"Did everything go okay at the tax place?" A fine thread of anxiety laced Hailey's question.

"We're good, squirt. Nothing for you to worry about."

Janelle noticed that Adam's dismissal of Hailey's concerns hadn't wiped the frown from her forehead.

"The IRS man was very nice," Janelle said. "He accepted the revised tax forms. Your dad will still owe a small amount of money but not nearly as much as we had feared." Adam had been so thrilled and relieved with the result of the meeting, he'd nearly danced out of the office. And then he'd kissed her. Since that moment his mood had taken a sharp downward turn.

"Like I said." Adam gave Hailey a thumbs-up. "We're good as gold."

Hailey visibly relaxed. Janelle was pretty sure Adam had no idea how perceptive his daughter was or how much she learned from conversations around her. A born worrier, she no doubt picked up vibes from her father in the tone of his voice or a troubled expression. She was becoming a very intuitive young lady. Adam appeared oblivious to that trait in his daughter. Down the road, that could be a huge mistake.

When asked how things went at Mrs. Murphy's

house, Hailey revealed after lunch that Mrs. Murphy had taken them into town for an ice-cream cone.

Janelle twisted in her seat to see Raeanne. "What kind of cone did you have, sweetie?"

Raeanne grinned. "Strawberry," she whispered.

Hailey's heart lurched at the sound of Rae's voice. One more word spoken aloud. One more small step forward. "Bet it was yummy."

Still grinning, her eyes twinkling, Rae rubbed her tummy and nodded.

Janelle was tempted to ask Adam to stop at the Pee Wee Drive-In to get the girls another cone just so she could encourage Raeanne to speak yet another word. Or maybe a whole phrase. But that would be foolish and certainly wouldn't encourage good eating habits.

Besides, since her disagreement with Adam, Janelle's stomach had felt pretty unsettled, and she didn't think it was from car sickness.

Once back home, Adam totally ignored Janelle. He quickly changed his clothes and went back to work in the garage.

Since the girls were engaged in playing with Kitty Cat, Janelle took the opportunity to change out of her suit and put on something more casual.

Emotionally drained, she sat on the deck in the Adirondack chair and closed her eyes. She hadn't meant to upset him. Adam had made it clear he wanted no help from her or anyone else. Feeling impotent and stymied in her effort to do what she knew ought to be done was frustrating.

Adam didn't have a monopoly on taking action.

But what could she do to help him that wouldn't raise his ire?

Maybe she ought to simply move out to a motel rather than stay here, a thorn in his side. A challenge to his ego and his self-esteem. But she'd never been a quitter.

When she'd first married Raymond, he had persisted in wearing ill-fitting clothes that made him look like a doddering old professor. To fix the problem, she'd gone shopping. Little by little, she'd improved his wardrobe. After that she'd worked on him to improve his hairstyle.

She gnawed on her lower lip. Apparently she'd improved his appearance so much that young coeds all across the country had found him attractive. Clearly he had not rejected their attention.

"Janelle?"

She started at Hailey's voice. "Yes, honey?"

"I just wondered…" A frown creased her young forehead. "Did you and Dad have an argument or something?"

A very perceptive girl. "The meeting with the IRS was a little stressful, but we're fine." Not a full answer, but one she thought would ease Hailey's mind.

"You sure? He seemed kind of grumpy. I thought maybe you two—"

Janelle slipped her arm around Hailey's waist and tugged her closer. "Your dad has a lot on his mind. He was probably thinking about some broken-down car he needed to put back together because he'd promised the owner he'd be finished by tonight."

Hailey didn't appear totally convinced. "It's just that I like you and Rae living here and all. If you and Dad got into a fight, you'd probably leave." She lifted her narrow shoulders in a helpless shrug.

Kissing Hailey on the forehead, Janelle hugged the child again. "We like it here, too. But you know at some point we'll have to move to a house of our own."

"I know. I just don't want it to be too soon."

A lump formed in Janelle's throat. A part of Janelle was as reluctant to leave as Hailey was to have her go. Which made her one very foolish woman.

After an early dinner, Adam drove Hailey to a friend's house for a birthday party and sleepover. Raeanne hadn't been invited, nor would Janelle have let her go. She was much too young, her emotions still too fragile, for Janelle to feel comfortable with Rae that far out of her sight.

"Don't look so glum, sweetie." Her daughter's lower lip was puffed out as if she'd been stung by a bee. "Hailey will be back home in the morning."

Head down, shoulders slumped, Rae walked over to the couch and climbed up in Janelle's lap.

"That's my girl. I know you're lonely, but we still have each other." She hugged her baby girl tight to her chest. Adam's coldness toward her had dampened her spirits, as well. "I know what we can do. Where are those library books? We'll have to take them back soon. Why don't we read them again?"

With a minimum of enthusiasm, Rae slid off her lap and went to retrieve them from the cottage.

When she returned, Janelle said, "Okay, up you come. Which book shall we read first?"

Raeanne handed her *The Owl and the Pussy Cat* and Janelle began to read. She'd gone through two other books and returned to the first one when she realized Rae was nearly asleep.

And there was still no sign of Adam. Was he avoiding her? Or had something gone wrong? An accident? Maybe a flat tire?

She shook her head. If he wanted to keep his distance, so be it. And if there was an accident, she'd hear about it soon enough.

"Up you go, Rae." She eased her sleepy daughter off her lap. "It's bedtime. Do you want to carry Kitty Cat, or should I?"

Raeanne decided that was her job. Picking up Kitty Cat from the chair where she had been dozing, she carried the kitten to the cottage. The nap had apparently re-energized Kitty Cat, because she leaped up onto the bed and buried herself under a corner of the quilt. Her little head peeked out. She meowed as though saying, "I'm ready for playtime."

"Silly Kitty Cat." Janelle helped Raeanne undress and put on her pajamas. "I don't think she knows it's bedtime."

When Raeanne climbed into bed, Janelle sat next to her for evening prayers. Rae folded her hands and closed her eyes.

"Now I lay me down to sleep. I pray the Lord my soul to keep. Wake me to the morning light. Watch over me all day and all night, and keep me safe." Janelle added prayers for others. "Watch over Mommy and Kitty Cat. Who else shall we pray for tonight?"

"Hailey," Rae whispered.

"Good. And watch over Hailey and her father." Janelle sent up her own personal prayer that the Lord would help Adam find peace within himself and seek help for his dyslexia. "We ask this in Jesus's name. Amen.

"I love you, Raeanne, more than the moon and the stars and the sky." She kissed Rae's cheek. "Nighty-night, sweet girl. I'll leave the night light on, but if you need me, I'll be on the deck or in the big house. I'll come to bed pretty soon. Okay?"

Sleepy-eyed, Rae nodded, and Janelle slipped out of the room.

She didn't feel much like sitting in the empty house and watching TV alone. The Adirondack chair tempted her as it so often had since she'd arrived at Adam's house. Sitting down, she leaned back to gaze at the stars. She should have picked up an astronomy book at the library so she could tell one star from another. Maybe she would tomorrow. Adam had said he'd teach her. But that was before she'd confronted him about his problem.

She heard the sliding door behind her open. Felt him step onto the deck.

"I wondered where everyone had gone."

"I just put Rae to bed. Did you get Hailey to her friend's all right?"

"Yeah. I stopped at the diner to have coffee with a couple of friends."

"Oh." She had no claim on Adam. He didn't have to report his whereabouts to her. Despite that, she did wish he'd let her know he'd be late. It was only reasonable she'd worry about him. At least a little.

"Mind if I sit down?"

"Of course not. It's your deck."

His jacket made a swishing noise as he sat in the

neighboring chair. "There's a touch of autumn in the air tonight. You ought to have a sweater on."

She folded her arms against a sudden rush of goose bumps. "I'm all right. I'll be going in soon."

He was quiet for a moment. "I'm sorry I jumped down your throat earlier. Guess I'm a little sensitive about my, um, problem."

"You don't have to be with me. I understand." Although she didn't understand why he hadn't tried to get help. Or why he was so ashamed of something that wasn't his fault. There must be hundreds of thousands of people in the country who suffered at some level for their inability to read.

He remained quiet as she listened to the rustling of small creatures moving through the underbrush and the distant call of an owl.

"I'd better go check on Rae. I'll see you in the morning."

He stood. "I'll walk you to the cottage."

Her brows lifted. Was this his way of making amends? "All right."

She opened the cottage door a crack. To her surprise, she heard Raeanne talking very softly. Curious, she peeked inside.

"Now, Kitty Cat, you and me and Ruff are having a sleepover. That means you have to go to sleep. No more playing."

In the glow of the night-light, Janelle saw Raeanne cover the kitten with a blanket.

"Now you say your prayers. Now I lay me down and my soul goes to sleep. Amen." She stretched out on the bed beside her kitty. "I love you, Kitty Cat, more than the moon and stars and sky."

Smiling, with tears in her eyes, Janelle took a step back and closed the door. Adam's arm came around her.

"She's talking," he said.

"Yes. She's finding her voice again. I've prayed so hard…"

She swallowed a sob, and he pulled her hard against his chest. He had no idea how much she needed to be held. To feel his strength around her. To believe that he'd forgiven her for discovering his secret.

It was going to be so hard to leave the man who had helped restore her daughter's voice, and his child, whom she had grown to love.

But would she be given a choice?

Chapter Ten

Before she went to bed, Janelle emailed her friend Eileen in Seattle. Hopefully she'd have a few ideas for helping Adam's dyslexia that weren't too intrusive.

Her friend's response came quickly. Although Eileen pointed out there were several types of dyslexia, and no reading program was guaranteed to help, she made several suggestions Janelle could easily implement after only a trip to the general store. Janelle planned to do that following the next day's edition of house hunting with Sharon.

When she returned home from her morning excursion, Hailey and Rae were playing a game of grocery shopping in the playhouse, which was well in sight of the garage and under Adam's watchful eye. They were using canned goods from the kitchen cupboard as props and "paying" for their purchases with water-smoothed stones from the beach.

She told the girls to come in for lunch. After seeing that they were fed, she made a sandwich for Adam, which she carried out to the garage along with the office supplies she'd purchased in town. Supplies she hoped would help Adam manage his business finances more easily.

He was leaning against an SUV that he'd been working on. "You're back."

"Sharon took me up to Kalispell to look at a couple of places."

He straightened abruptly. "That's in a big, flat valley and the town is mobbed by more tourists than even we get."

"True. But they do have a large school district. The housing prices aren't much different than here in Bear Lake."

"Maybe so." His scowled deepened and he shoved a hand into the pocket of his overalls. "But I sure wouldn't want to live there."

"I brought you a sandwich." She placed it on the side of the desk and sat down in his swivel chair, putting her supply of file folders, colored markers and tabs she'd purchased on the desk. "I decided I liked Bear Lake better, too, but it was worth the trip." Someday soon she'd have to take that ride over the Going-to-the-Sun Road that crossed through Glacier National Park. The views had to be spectacular.

"Besides, Sharon reassured me about the local school district here. I was worried when you told me about your experiences. Turns out they now have a reading specialist on staff, and a family and child counselor is on call from Kalispell. She says the test scores are above average for the state." Because Rae was so bright, Janelle definitely wanted her to have a superior education. And if she needed further counseling, it was good to know a therapist was on call.

"I could've told you the local schools are good." He wiped his hands and came into the office to eat. "So you're going to stick with Bear Lake?"

"Assuming I can find a house I like." One that Adam didn't shoot down as being inappropriate for one reason or another. She'd begun to suspect a pattern in his complaints about her housing options. So far, she wasn't quite sure why. He didn't need a full-time bookkeeper on the premises. Hailey having a young playmate kept her out of Adam's hair, but that would be less important once school started. She'd have her friends to play with and homework to do.

"It's good you're looking here." He took a bite of his sandwich. "This is great," he said around a mouthful of sliced chicken.

"I used a Dijon mustard with a bit of dill to brighten the flavor." She spread out her supplies on the desk. "I've thought of an easier way for you to keep your records straight. I'm going to color-code the file folders. I'll use a red tab like this—" she showed him "—for the folder of bills to be paid."

He kept eating the sandwich, but a frown appeared, drawing his brows together.

"When the bill is paid, it goes into the file folder with the blue tab. That's sort of a soothing color, which seems right for a bill you don't have to worry about any longer."

He nodded but without a lot of enthusiasm.

"Your bank statements go in the green-tab folder. Money is green, right?"

"Logical," he mumbled. "You're doing this because I'm dyslexic."

"I'm doing this to make the record-keeping easier for you and me. There are lots of people who aren't dyslexic who color-code their records. It makes sense to have a system that lets you go right to the file you want."

"If you say so."

Stubborn man! She picked up an envelope that had been delivered that morning in the mail and pulled out the credit-card statement. "Now then, when you receive an invoice, you use one of these markers in the corner. Since this is a bill, you tick the corner with the red marker."

He eyed her warily. "Then it goes in the red folder."

"Perfect." She leaned back in her chair wondering if it was sarcasm she'd heard in his voice or indignation. She wasn't trying to insult him or his intelligence. Color-coding records made sense for everyone. "After you pay the bill and note the check number, you make another tick mark in blue because you don't have to worry about it anymore. Until tax time, of course."

He finished the last of his sandwich and brushed the crumbs from his hands. "So where did you get this bright idea?"

She tried for a casual shrug. "I worked part-time in an office while I was going to college. Up to the time I got married, anyway. Raymond didn't want me to work outside the home." Which, in retrospect, was a mistake, she realized. She should have had her own life and career instead of focusing all of her energy on Raymond, and later Raeanne. Not that she regretted a moment she'd spent with her daughter, but she would be in a much better position for job hunting if she had some recent experience on her resume. "Color-coding files isn't exactly a new idea." As Eileen had reminded her in the email.

"Okay. I guess that'll work."

"I know the tax problem has been resolved, but if you still want me to work for you part-time, I could spend a couple of half days per week keeping the records up-to-date, paying the bills and giving you monthly reports of income versus expenses."

"Then I wouldn't need to fuss with all that color-coding business."

She gritted her teeth and rolled her eyes. Why on earth was he so resistant to a change that would make life easier for him? Was it his pride? Or plain bullheadedness?

"This change would be a big improvement over you simply tossing everything into a pile." She could be bullheaded, too, and she let it show in her voice. "Maybe you'd actually be able to find something yourself."

He pushed himself up from the chair. "Okay. Do what you want. As far as I'm concerned, you're in charge. A bunch of colored tabs aren't going to change the fact that I can't read worth beans and will never be able to."

He marched back to the SUV, climbed inside and started the engine. A moment later he had his head stuck under the hood. A perfect place to hide from his problems.

So much for Eileen's idea number one.

Humph! If Adam thought she was done trying to help him, he was wrong. There was more than one way to tame a stubborn man.

That evening after the girls were in bed, Adam grabbed his telescope and tripod. He wandered out onto the deck and set up his gear. A good, clear night for stargazing. He spotted Ophiuchus and trained his scope on the house-shaped constellation, adjusting the focus.

He didn't need any color-coded gimmicks or contrivances to find stars in the night sky. Janelle must think he was the stupidest guy in the world to believe she'd come up with that idea to make things easier for *her*. She did it for him. And he resented her efforts to change who he was.

Lisa had accepted and loved him just as he was, warts and all. Except she'd warned him not to let anyone know he couldn't read for fear he'd lose business and embarrass her and Hailey.

Janelle was going to try to "fix" him just like his third-grade teacher who kept him after school every day trying to pound reading into his head. But no matter how much she pushed and cajoled, told him he could learn to read like other kids, the letters kept jumping around as if they were Mexican jumping beans.

He'd tried! He hadn't wanted to be stupid. No

kid would ask for that. But the best he'd ever done was get a couple of words to stick together long enough for him to figure out what they meant.

Then the letters would split apart to do a jitter-bug dance on the page.

As an adult, things hadn't gotten much better. He was just better at disguising the problem. Faking it. Finding ways to work around it.

Except Janelle hadn't taken long to see right through his phony excuses. Why couldn't she just leave him alone?

Except that wasn't what he wanted, either.

He liked having her around. He liked how she treated his daughter and how Hailey responded to her.

He liked how she felt when he held her. When he kissed her.

But for Adam, she was off-limits. He had to remember that. Keep his distance.

His grip tightened on the telescope. Every day, despite Janelle's determination to fix him, it got harder and harder to imagine what it would be like when she was no longer a part of his life.

Her working part-time wasn't going to be enough to satisfy him. He wanted more—a real, lasting relationship. But he didn't dare set his sights that high. He'd only be disappointed when she rejected him.

He heard her walking toward him on the boardwalk from the cottage. He closed his eyes, blocking out the stars in the constellation Ophiuchus and picturing the sparkle in her eyes when she laughed.

"That's quite a telescope you've got." She stopped near him, close enough that he caught the scent of her fruity shampoo on the night air.

He lifted his head away from the eyepiece. "You should see my dad's. It's five times more powerful. He liked the idea of moving to Arizona so he could take it up in the mountains and set up his own observatory."

"It's nice he has a hobby like that."

"I think my mom gets a little tired of him going off with his amateur astronomer buddies, but she has friends there now, so they're okay." He gestured toward the telescope. "You want to take a look?"

She stepped around and put her eye to the scope. "What am I looking at?"

"The constellation of Ophiuchus. It's about nine stars—not all of them are as bright as the others. They form a shape that looks like the outline of a house drawn by a kindergartner. It's kind of lying on its side."

She stared into the scope for a minute and then

lifted her head. "I don't see anything that looks like a house."

He checked to see the scope was still focused properly.

"Okay, let's see if I can help you spot it without the telescope. Then you'll know what you're looking for." He stepped behind her, his head close to hers, her hair soft against his cheek. He pointed toward the constellation. "The top of the roof is the brightest star. Do you see that?"

"I guess so." She didn't move and neither did he.

"Now, if you slide down the roof on the left side to another star that's not quite so bright, you'll just be able to make out a dimmer star that's like the eave on the house."

When he inhaled, strands of her hair tickled his cheek.

"Yes, I think I've got that."

"Okay, let's look in the scope again. See if you can find that part of Ophiuchus."

She shifted back to the scope. "Oh, I see it! That first star is really bright and so close. I had no idea." A smile of excitement lifted her voice.

Still standing next to her, close enough that he could have swept those same strands of hair back over her delicate ear, he described the stars that formed the rest of the outline.

"That's how my dad taught me to see Ophiuchus. But actually it's supposed to represent a man holding a serpent."

"What?" She back away from the scope. "A serpent?"

"I know. It doesn't look like that to me, either. Maybe whoever named the stars didn't have a kid in kindergarten."

She laughed, and the sound rippled around him, warming him like a winter coat.

How would he ever be able to let her go?

Yet if she couldn't change him, fix his problem, there'd be no way for him to keep her. Dyslexia was a part of him. Who he was. It wasn't fixable.

He knew because he'd tried. Because he'd prayed to God when he was a kid that he'd wake up in the morning and be able to read.

Never happened. Not going to happen now.

After helping her locate a couple more constellations, they sat down in the Adirondack chairs to enjoy the night sounds.

"I'm curious," Adam commented. "What did you do as an anthropologist with your husband?"

"Raymond's specialty was the study of bears as symbols in various cultures."

"Bears? Like Smokey the Bear?"

"More or less. He spent a part of every summer living with some remote native tribe gathering information about how they viewed bears."

"Why?" That sounded like a waste of time to Adam, but who was he to say?

She laughed. "A lot of people used to ask him that question. Usually he'd go into a long dissertation on the subject that would put the questioner right to sleep."

That wouldn't take long in Adam's case. "Did you go with him to these villages?"

"Only once. I caught some dreadful intestinal disease and he sent me home." A note of regret seeped into her voice.

"You must still miss him."

She was silent for a moment before she replied. "After Raymond died, I discovered he hadn't been faithful to me. Turned out all my efforts to improve his appearance from a stodgy professor to a well-dressed professional worked well to attract young coeds he met on his lecture circuit." Her laughter held a bitter edge. "So rather than grieving, I got angry at him. I still am, but mostly now because he'd never spent the time to really get to know Raeanne."

"That's a hard one to swallow. But I've gotta tell you, any man who'd be unfaithful to you would have to be an idiot."

In the starlight, he saw her smile. "Thank you."

Her words were no more than a whisper on the wind, but Adam felt them curl around his heart.

He could guarantee, if he were Janelle's husband, he'd never stray from home and hearth. Not ever.

Not that he had a chance of marrying her. Even so, he secretly acknowledged he was glad she wasn't still grieving over the loss of her husband.

Sunday brought with it renewed heat and the threat of an afternoon thunderstorm.

As Janelle walked toward the church, she glanced up at the clouds gathering over the mountains. "Maybe we should have brought our umbrellas," she said to Adam.

"Nah. We'll be home long before those clouds drop any rain on us."

They hadn't quite reached the door when Adrienne Walker, the pastor's wife, hurried out to meet them.

"Janelle, I'm so glad you came to church this morning." Breathless, she placed her hand over her chest. "Our soprano soloist has laryngitis. She can't sing a note. Sounds like a frog, the poor dear. Could you please, *please* fill in for her? Our second soprano doesn't have a strong enough voice to carry the solo and I don't know—"

"Mrs. Walker, I can't sing a solo when I haven't rehearsed with the choir." Janelle quailed at the very thought. "I don't even know what hymn you're singing. Or if it's in my key. I couldn't possibly—"

"Do call me Adrienne, dear. It's not a long solo,

and I'm sure you're familiar with the hymn. It's one of my favorites."

She named a tune Janelle was at least acquainted with, but not one she'd ever sung except as a member of the congregation.

"We have a guest preacher from headquarters this morning," Adrienne continued. "I know it's one of his favorite hymns, too, and we so don't want to disappoint him. Please?"

"Go ahead," Adam said. "Give it a shot. What could go wrong?"

Her mouth went dry, and her eyes darted around in search of escape. Sweat formed under her arms. "I could embarrass myself and the whole choir. That's what could go wrong."

"I've heard you sing, dear. I promise you won't embarrass yourself."

Janelle's gazed landed on Raeanne. "But I can't leave my daughter. She's doesn't like—"

"I'll watch her," Adam said.

"I'll skip Sunday School and sit with her," Hailey volunteered. "I think you ought to do it. My mom used to say you should take advantage of the opportunities God gives you."

Mentally, Janelle groaned. *Out of the mouths of babes.*

Adrienne slipped her arm through Janelle's. "Come along, dear. I'll show you where we keep the choir robes and you can run through some scales and warm up backstage."

Janelle realized Adrienne's successful volunteer-recruitment technique involved coercion. "I don't—" She rubbed her cheek, tugged on her earlobe and looked at Raeanne. "Will you be all right sitting with Adam and Hailey?"

The child responded with an eager nod of her head.

A whole swarm of butterflies took flight in Janelle's stomach. Far more butterflies than she'd ever experienced when she'd had the lead in her high-school musical.

"You know you may be sorry you asked me to do this," she warned the minister's wife.

"Never. The Lord has blessed you with a beautiful voice. He won't let you down now."

Janelle prayed Adrienne was right. This might be the one time God had made a serious mistake in judgment.

The first two songs the choir sang were familiar, and the soprano part carried the melody, so Janelle was able to blend her voice with the rest of the choir. But as they drew closer to singing the hymn with the soprano solo, she literally began to sweat. The music folder trembled in her hands.

Adrienne leaned toward her. "Your voice is a

gift from God. Use it to sing praise unto the Lord and He will be standing beside you."

Janelle stood on cue with the choir. The organist played the opening notes. Janelle filled her lungs with air and her heart with faith in the Lord. *Please let me be a reflection of Your love.*

She began to sing. Hesitantly at first. Then with more confidence and power. Her voice soared toward the heavens. The choir joined in and she fused her voice with theirs again, sending up a prayer of thanksgiving.

As soon as the service was completed and the choir had retreated to the dressing room, the members descended on her with hugs and congratulations.

"What a lovely voice."

"Please do join the choir."

"You'll be at choir practice Thursday night, won't you?"

Stunned by their reaction, she hedged, unwilling to make a promise she might not be able to keep. She didn't want to fail these warm, friendly people who had made her feel so welcome.

With a grateful smile, a few words of thanks and knees that were still shaking, she escaped outside, where the parishioners were gathered to chat with friends. She craned her neck in search of Adam. But before she could spot him, members of the congregation surrounded her, overwhelming her with congratulations. Her cheeks flamed hot with all of the attention and praise they heaped on her.

"Hey, Janie, over here."

She heard Adam's voice, and relief surged through her. She quickly excused herself to join Adam and the girls.

Raeanne gave her a big hug around her waist.

"Hi, sweetie. Were you good for Adam in church?"

"She was perfect," Adam said. "Weren't you, Buttercup?"

Raeanne giggled.

"That was a beautiful solo, Janelle." Hailey's eyes shone with shared pride. "Did you hear everybody clapping for you?"

"No, I…" She'd heard nothing after her solo except the other choir members and a roaring in her ears.

"Daddy clapped the loudest," Hailey said.

Adam shrugged. "Seemed the thing to do. You were pretty awesome."

His praise touched her in a way no one else's had and brought tears to her eyes. "Thank you."

A well-dressed woman in her sixties approached them. "Excuse me. I'm Doris Jackson, and this is my husband, Ed." She drew her husband closer. "First, I wanted to tell you how much we enjoyed your singing."

Drawing Raeanne closer to her, Janelle nodded her appreciation. "Thank you."

"Adrienne mentioned that you were looking for a house to buy in Bear Lake," Doris said.

"That's true." Not quite sure why Doris was so interested, Janelle maintained her smile.

"We've decided to move to Denver. That's where our children are now, and we'd like to be near them and our grandchildren. We just listed our house with Sharon Brevik at Lake Country Real Estate, but if you'd like to take a look, we'd love to have you drop by."

Janelle caught a glimpse of Adam's sudden scowl. Was he already gearing up to find fault with the Jackson house as he had with others that had interested her? Was the house sitting on top of an oil pipeline? Or perhaps it was the victim of some other negative feature she hadn't even imagined.

"It's three bedrooms with a daylight basement you could use as a playroom and formal dining room," Ed interjected. "A good family home and just blocks from the school. We raised our three kids there."

"Then I'm sure you have many fond memories of your home," Janelle said.

Ed handed her a business card. "Come on by to take a look when you have a chance."

"We like the idea of someone like you living in our place and taking good care of it," Doris added.

"That's very thoughtful of you. I'll drop by soon."

Adam took her arm. "We'd better get going before those clouds let loose."

Looking up, Janelle realized the clouds she'd seen earlier were racing overhead, and they looked ominous. Just then, a lightning bolt streaked its way across the sky.

Before she could say goodbye to the Jacksons, Adam began tugging her toward the truck. Almost manhandling her.

She shrugged out of his grasp.

What was wrong with him? Every time the conversation turned to her buying a house, he went all grumpy and possessive on her. Surely he didn't intend for her and Raeanne to live in the cottage indefinitely?

Theirs was a temporary arrangement. That's all he had offered and the only agreement she had made.

With a firm resolve, she forcefully ignored the possibility that their one kiss might be the prelude to more.

Chapter Eleven

Thunder and lightning raged across the sky. A waterfall of rain pounded on the deck, splashing the sliding glass door.

Inside, Adam had started a fire as soon as they'd gotten home from church, and the house was cozy and warm. The girls were on the floor in front of the fireplace playing Candy Land. Janelle was working at the kitchen table creating a fall wreath with the dried flowers, wild grass and pinecones they'd gathered at their picnic.

Lightning flashed again, almost immediately followed by a clap of thunder. Janelle flinched, and the girls looked up from their game.

"Let me tell you, they don't get storms like this in Seattle."

Adam shot her a lopsided grin. "This is nothing. You should see it when it really gets worked up."

She wasn't eager to witness a storm worse than

this one. She wasn't afraid of thunder and lightning. Not exactly. But they sure put her on edge and made her jittery. Like a good mom, though, she tried not to let her nerves show.

"We may lose power if this keeps up," he said. "If we do, I'll turn on the generator. In a bad storm, trees can blow over on the power lines and the whole town can be without electricity for several days."

"Several days? Does everyone have a generator?" She wondered what one would cost and if she'd have any idea how to run it.

"Most do, particularly the businesses. I can remember some great parties at the Pine Tree Inn when the power was out."

Janelle could only wonder about what kind of parties he enjoyed.

Apparently finished with their board game, Raeanne got up and brought Janelle a picture book to read.

She glanced toward Adam, who appeared fascinated by the falling rain outside. This might be a good opportunity to try another one of Eileen's ideas.

"Sweetie, I'm busy making this wreath. Why don't you ask Adam to read you the story?"

Raeanne seemed happy with the idea. Adam wasn't. The angry look he sent her was enough to singe the roots of her hair. She responded to his glowering with a friendly, innocent smile, which she was sure he didn't appreciate.

Still sitting on the floor, Hailey opened her mouth to say something, but when Janelle gave a quick shake of her head, she remained silent.

Not waiting for a further invitation, Rae climbed up beside Adam in the big leather recliner. Despite his displeasure with Janelle, he made room for her daughter.

A moment later, Kitty Cat sauntered into the room and jumped up in Raeanne's lap, curling into a tiny, colorful ball of fur.

"I don't know, Rae," Adam said. "I bet you know this story better than I do."

"I have something that will make reading the book more fun." Janelle slipped a sheet of red cellophane from her craft box. According to Eileen, people with dyslexia were often bothered by black letters on a white background. They could see the letters with less strain when they read through colored cellophane. "You can pretend the princess lives in an exciting world where the sky is always red."

She opened the book, which was in Adam's lap, and put the cellophane in place.

"See how fun that looks?" Her throat tightened on the false sincerity and she mentally crossed her fingers. She so hoped this would help him decipher the letters and words more easily.

Electricity from an internal storm seemed to shimmer through the air as he glared at her, then looked down at the page. "Yeah, right. Lots of fun."

Raeanne snuggled more closely against him.

"Okay, Buttercup. Let's see what kind of a story we've got here. What's this?"

"Princess," Rae whispered.

"That's right. And she lives in a big ole castle." He pointed again. "Who's this?"

"Prince."

Janelle backed slowly away. Adam wasn't actually reading the book. Instead he was reading the pictures. But amazingly, Raeanne was speaking. She'd heard the book read so many times, she knew the characters and the story. Together they were making it work.

Returning to her wreath making, Janelle kept an eye on Adam. He seemed to be puzzling over the words. Not saying them out loud but giving them a close examination. Maybe, just maybe…

Hailey sat down at the kitchen table across from Janelle. Picking up a bundle of dried flowers, she studied them carefully. "My mother was usually the one who read books to me."

Janelle heard a hint of question in the child's

voice, and her expression held both worry and fear. "It's a very special thing moms do, reading to their children."

"My dad does other things that are special."

"I know. I've seen what a good father he is. You're very lucky to have him for your dad." She wove a trio of purple wildflowers into the wreath's backing, which she had made out of two wire coat hangers bent into a circle and covered with floral tape.

"It was okay that he never read me a book when I was little. We used to build Lego sets together. He's real good at that."

"I'm sure he is. That's why he's such a terrific mechanic."

"A long time ago he made me the swing set and playhouse. Once he made a tree house, but a storm blew the tree down." She shrugged as though it didn't matter.

"I never had a tree house. Bet they're fun." Janelle was, however, increasingly confident that Hailey knew her father wasn't able to read, at least not as well as he should. She might not be familiar with the term *dyslexia,* but she knew and was defending her dad. Protecting a secret she wasn't supposed to know.

"And they lived happily ever after in the land of the red sky!" Adam boomed the climax of the book, and Raeanne clapped.

He eased himself out of the chair. "Hey, Peanut, come read Rae another book, would you?"

Hailey gave Janelle a hard look, almost a warning, then went into the living room to find a new book.

As casual as you please, Adam strolled into the kitchen, opened the refrigerator and took out a can of soda. "What was that all about?" he asked with his back still turned to Janelle, his voice low and accusing.

"I'd read somewhere that using colored cellophane could help a person read more easily." She kept her voice equally low, almost intimate.

"A dyslexic person." He spit out the words in a harsh whisper.

"Yes. Did it help any?"

He slammed the refrigerator door and whirled toward her. A muscle flexed in his jaw. He popped the top on the can, drank a big gulp of the cola and set the can firmly on the table.

"I don't know."

She blinked. He didn't know? How could he not tell one way or the other whether the cellophane had helped?

"Sometimes colors other than red work better. Yellow. A pale blue."

They spoke in quiet voices barely above a whisper so they wouldn't be overheard.

"I don't want any other colors." He walked

to the sink and looked outside. The worst of the storm had passed, leaving only a steady rainfall behind. "The letters didn't jump around as much as they usually do."

Janelle wanted to leap up and click her heels together, but she restrained her excitement. "Then it helped."

"A little," he said grudgingly.

"There are other things you can try. There are even online classes with individual counseling and assistance. They don't cost too much."

"I already told you to keep out of my business. I have no intention of sitting around the house all day staring at a computer screen."

"It only takes a half hour per day," she countered.

When he started to walk out of the kitchen, she stepped in front of him and placed her hand in the middle of his chest right over his heart. A pulse throbbed in his throat. He might not like it, would probably resent it, but she had to tell him about Hailey.

"Your daughter knows you can't read."

His eyes narrowed, the irises darkening until there was very little gray remaining. "You're lying."

She grimaced at his accusation. It hurt that he'd think she would lie to him. "No, I'm not. Twice now, first when I asked her if you needed glasses and now when I cornered you into reading to Rae, she's become very defensive. She's trying to help you keep your secret. But she knows the truth."

His gaze left hers, ricocheting to Hailey in the living room. "She couldn't know."

"She's a very intelligent girl. Living with you, observing you every day of her life, she knows, all right. But she doesn't understand why it's a secret. Neither do I."

Janelle watched the stubborn jut of his chin and the defiant look in his eyes melt away. "I can't tell her. She'll think—"

"She'll be relieved to have it out in the open. I promise you, she won't think badly of you, and there's no reason for you to be ashamed. It's a neurological problem and has nothing to do with your intelligence. She loves you very much. You're her dad. There shouldn't be any secrets between you."

He leaned very close to her, close enough that she could feel his heat. And his anger. "I'm not going to tell Hailey, and neither are you."

With that he brushed past her and into the living room. "Hey, Hailey, why don't we work on one of the gigantic jigsaw puzzles you've got? Seems like a perfect thing to do on a rainy afternoon. Remember how your mom loved to work on those things for hours and hours?"

Hailey seemed thrilled with the idea. She raced off to her room and came running back with a five-hundred-piece puzzle that she dumped onto the dining table.

Janelle was far less thrilled. Adam was still dodging his problem. Covering it up. If he continued to pretend that no one, including Hailey, knew he couldn't read then he'd only be fooling himself.

If he didn't come clean soon, before his daughter was much older, Janelle feared he'd have a price to pay.

Adam didn't have anywhere to hide.

As he bent over the jigsaw puzzle trying to piece it together, he could still feel Janelle's hand branding his chest with disapproval. Now he felt her eyes burrowing into his back, prodding him to come clean. To reveal to his own daughter that he couldn't read the words in a picture book. To agree to Janelle's idea of taking an online class so he'd no longer need to feel ashamed.

Hailey kept behaving oddly, too. Quick glances toward him and then she'd look back at the puzzle just as fast, avoiding eye contact. She couldn't know about his dyslexia. If she did, she would have said something. Wouldn't she?

Kids were like sponges. They sopped up information. But then they blurted out whatever they saw or heard. She wouldn't keep his disability to herself, would she? If she'd overheard Adam and her mom talking about dyslexia, she would have said something. Asked questions.

She sure asked questions about everything else under the sun.

"Dad, that blue piece is part of the sky. Don't put it in the middle of the tree."

"Oh." He pulled back the piece. "It looked like it might fit."

"Not in the tree." She selected another piece that fit perfectly and was the right color.

Okay, so he wasn't great at jigsaw puzzles. That was Lisa's deal. But he could put together a model car or a full-size carburetor in minutes and didn't need the directions. That ought to count for something.

Even more important, he loved his daughter more than life itself. He didn't want to disappoint her. If she found out he couldn't read, it would shatter her opinion of him. Make her love him less.

Unless she already knew the truth.

He glanced over his shoulder toward Janelle, and a knot twisted in his gut. What if she was right?

That night when he went to bed he couldn't sleep. He kept thinking back to the story he'd read to Rae. Had that stupid sheet of cellophane made a difference? Or had he imagined the letters weren't hopping around on the page as much as usual?

That made no sense. Whatever he thought was

happening, it had to have been an illusion. Maybe he'd realized Janelle was messing around with some gimmick she'd heard about. Maybe subconsciously he'd wanted the slick trick to work.

But it couldn't have been real.

He sat up and swung his legs over the side of the bed. The house was quiet. Hailey had been asleep for hours. Janelle and Rae were safely tucked away in the cottage.

He could get a glass of milk in the kitchen. Stretch out the kinks in his neck. And then get to sleep so he wouldn't be totally wiped out tomorrow.

After the storm a cold front had moved through the area, so he pulled on his robe but didn't bother to find his slippers. He padded barefoot into the kitchen and switched on the light over the counter.

Janelle had left her box of craft supplies on the counter along with the wreath she was making. The pinecones she'd wired in among the dried flowers looked real nice. Not only was she a classy lady, but she was artistic, too.

As he poured himself some milk, he noticed the sheets of cellophane laying on top of her supplies. A bunch of colors…red, pink, yellow, green. How weird was that? No way could any color help him to read.

Still, he looked around the living room. Rae had left her stack of picture books on the coffee table. Usually Janelle was good about getting her daughter to pick up her stuff and take it back to the cottage when they turned in for the night.

Maybe Janelle had been as upset as he was about the whole reading fiasco and had forgotten.

Leaving the milk on the counter, he walked into the living room. He picked up the book he'd "read" to Raeanne. Each page had only a couple of lines of text. The pictures pretty well told the story on their own.

Curious, and more than a little skeptical, he carried the book to the kitchen and put it on the counter under the light. He studied the first page of the story. The print was pretty big. Not like trying to read the fine print on an IRS form or credit-card bill. Or even an engine-repair manual.

Apparently size didn't matter. It took all the concentration he had to work out the words. *Once. Upon. A. Time.*

Great, he was reading at the kindergarten level.

Out of sheer spite, he grab a yellow sheet of cellophane and looked again. Not much help there. Green and blue didn't do much either. Then he slapped the red sheet on the page.

Once upon a time...

But he'd already figured out that part. The fact that the letters stayed in place meant nothing.

Except when he turned the page he read, "'In the land of the...morn...ing sun...'"

The phonics drills that the third-grade teacher had put him through crept back into his brain.

Suddenly he felt dizzy and glanced away from the page. His knees went weak. He grabbed his glass of milk and downed it in one gulp.

How was it possible?

Janelle made an appointment the following afternoon to go with Sharon Brevik to see the Jackson house. The trees still glistened with raindrops, but now the sky was a Wedgwood blue dotted by only a few lingering white, puffy clouds.

When she'd gotten up this morning, Adam had eaten breakfast and was already at work in the garage. Avoiding her, very likely.

Her interference, her pushing him about his dyslexia, had left her in an untenable position. She couldn't continue to live in his cottage if he refused to speak to her in anything more than single syllables and unintelligible grunts.

Pursing her lips, she admitted she'd ruined everything. The connection she'd felt with him. The spark of attraction that now they'd never have a chance to explore.

Even worse, Raeanne had made such huge strides in regaining her speech, largely due to Adam's influence. She worried that moving out now, combined with estrangement from Adam and his daughter, would set Raeanne's progress back again. Another loss in her child's life.

Janelle's fault. She should have left well enough alone. Despite his dyslexia, he was coping just fine with 99 percent of his life. Not everyone managed that well. That in itself was a very impressive accomplishment.

She turned off the highway into the Lake Country Realty parking lot. Sharon was right there to meet her.

"I'm ready to go if you are," Sharon said.

"I'm all set." She locked her car door and climbed into Sharon's car.

"You left the girls at home today," Sharon commented as she backed the car around and exited the gravel parking lot.

"Adam is at the garage. He seems to be okay keeping an eye on them."

"From what I've heard, he's doing great as a single father. Not that he wouldn't rather get married again and share the parenting duties, I'm sure. I guess the right woman hasn't come along yet." She glanced at Janelle and raised a questioning brow.

Janelle had no interest in satisfying Sharon's curiosity one way or the other.

"Tell me more about the Jackson house," she asked instead.

"Nice place and a good value. I think if they'd listed the property last spring or early summer they would have had a better chance of getting top dollar. This being so close to school starting and all, most folks are settled and not out house shopping."

Janelle wished she were already settled, but so far Adam had shot down every house she'd seriously considered buying. Perhaps now that he was upset with her, Adam wouldn't go so far out of his way to say something negative about the Jackson house.

The property was about a quarter mile west of the main part of Bear Lake and up on a hill with a distant view of the lake. It sat in the center of a partially wooded half-acre lot. Plenty of room to play along with adequate privacy, yet neighbors were within shouting distance. Overall, the house and grounds shouted *upscale!*

"Oh, my. I don't think this is in my price range." Janelle had seen enough listings, online and in person, to know the Jackson house was on the high end of her budget, if not over the top.

"Let's not worry about that yet. The Jacksons are flexible and eager to sell. They don't want to spend another winter here, and they love the idea that you attend their church."

The house itself was two stories with gray siding and dark green trim. The long porch across the front of the building looked like the place to watch the sunrise over the hills, and no doubt the back had a similar sunset view.

Sharon pulled to a stop in front of a two-car attached garage. "Pretty impressive, isn't it?"

"Very." Tempting, too, except without a full-time job, Janelle wasn't sure she could meet the monthly payments.

Ed and Doris Jackson met them at the door. They all exchanged hugs like longtime friends and Doris ushered them inside.

Immediately Janelle noticed how the house had been well loved and cared for by the Jacksons. Family snapshots were scattered about on end tables where a few dings reminded visitors of the children who'd been raised here and were now out on their own.

As she toured the house, Janelle noted that most of the rooms could use a new coat of paint, but basically the house was in very good condition. Her fingers itched to bake a cake or prepare a gourmet meal in the upgraded kitchen.

She turned to ask Sharon a question just as the Realtor's cell phone chimed.

"Oh, I'm sorry. I meant to turn my cell off." Sharon dug in her pocket.

"Go ahead, take the call. I'll check out the spare bedroom." An extra room would be great for her crafts. She could have a worktable that she could leave out and not have to clean up her mess when it was time for dinner.

Sharon followed her into the bedroom, her face pale. She extended the phone to Janelle.

"It's Adam. He didn't have your number. Something's happened to Raeanne."

Chapter Twelve

Janelle's breath lodged in her lungs as she took the phone from Sharon.

"What happened?" Her voice cracked. "Is Rae-anne—"

"Easy does it. The doctor says Rae's going to be fine."

"The doctor?" Her hand covered her mouth. Her legs gave out, and she sank down on the edge of the bed. Fighting a sweep of panic, she ordered herself to remain calm. "Where is she?"

"We're at Bear Lake Medical Clinic. The doctor wants to talk with you. Hang on."

Fear tightened her chest. Raeanne's injuries must be serious if Adam had taken her to the clinic.

"Mrs. Townsend, I'm Doctor Johansen, head of E.R. Your daughter's injury is not serious, but I do need your permission to treat her."

"Yes, of course." She swallowed a shaky sob.

"She has a head injury, a possible concussion and needs a few stitches."

"Do whatever you need to do."

"Thank you. I assume you'll be coming to the hospital."

"As soon as I can get there."

"Good. I'll see you shortly. Now I'll give the phone back to Adam."

Her whole body trembling, Janelle looked up at Sharon. "I have to get to Bear Lake Medical Clinic."

"I'll take you." Sharon took her arm. "Keep talking to Adam. It won't take us long to get there."

In a blur of dread and fear, Janelle let the Realtor make their excuses and they both hurried out of the house.

"I'm back," Adam said on the phone.

"Tell me what happened." With the phone still at her ear, Janelle got into the passenger seat of Sharon's car. Guilt assailed her. In all this time, she hadn't given Adam her phone number. What had she been thinking? At any time Janelle had been away from the house, Rae could have needed her, and there wouldn't have been any way to reach her. Thank God Adam had thought to call Sharon's number.

"The girls were playing around my boat at the end of the dock. I was on the deck watching them.

Somehow Raeanne must have slipped. She hit her head and fell into the water. Hailey jumped in after her before I could even get to her."

Nausea churned in her stomach. *Dear God, my baby! Please don't let me lose my baby.* "Was she unconscious?"

"Yes, for a short time. Hailey had pulled her out of the water and I carried her up onto the beach."

Bless them both!

"I put her in the car and drove here as fast as I could."

Sharon sped through an intersection and then made a sharp right turn. Janelle grabbed for a handhold.

"You didn't call the paramedics?" The words came out of her mouth like an accusation, but it was her fear speaking. Not her heart.

"It was faster to drive her here myself. Like the fire department, the medics are all volunteers. Sometimes it takes them a while to get to their unit and then to the scene where they're needed."

She'd have to thank him later for his quick thinking, and Hailey's, too, but right now her thoughts were entirely focused on getting to Raeanne as soon as she could. *I couldn't lose Raeanne. God would never be that cruel.*

Sharon roared up to a clinic entrance marked Emergency and slammed the car to a stop. "Give me your car keys. You go see to your little girl. I'll see to it your car gets back to Adam's place."

In a frenzy of fear and trepidation, Janelle found her keys, handed them to Sharon and blasted out of the car at a run. As soon as the automatic doors slid open, Adam was there waiting for her. Still wearing his grease-stained overalls, his eyes were bleak, the shape of his lips grim.

"I'm so sorry, Janie. I should've been right down there on the beach with them."

Beyond Adam, Hailey stood, looking forlorn and frightened. Her hair hung limp, and she'd been given a set of hospital scrubs to wear that were too big for her.

"Where's Rae? I want to see her. I want to see for myself—" She headed for the receptionist, but Adam snared her arm.

"She's in the emergency room. I told her you were coming." He eased her toward a door that said Authorized Personnel Only.

"Dad? Can I come with you?"

"Not now, Peanut. I'll come back out in a minute." He punched a buzzer and the E.R. door opened.

Vaguely aware of the smell of antiseptic and medications, Janelle rushed to the first of three cubicles. She swept back the curtain. Raeanne! Awake and looking right at her, her child-size body tiny compared to the long gurney. Her hair was still damp. She wore a child-size hospital gown, a blanket draped over her.

"Mommy?"

"Yes, sweetie, I'm here now." Relief and joy filled Janelle's chest at the sound of her daughter's soft voice and the sight of her big brown eyes. Tear tracks streaked her baby's cheeks. A row of stitches slashed across a swab of red on her forehead.

A doctor in a white jacket stood next to Raeanne, removing his latex gloves.

"Mrs. Townsend. I'm glad Adam was able to reach you. Your daughter's been a very fine and brave young lady."

Janelle barely acknowledged his comment. Instead, she went directly to the head of the gurney, bent over and kissed Raeanne.

"Oh, sweetie, what happened to you?" She caressed her daughter's soft cheek.

"I fell and got an owie, but Doctor Jason sewed me up. He said he could maybe come sew up Ruff's owies, too."

Tears born of the need to release her anxiety burned in Janelle's eyes. "That would be very nice of the doctor, wouldn't it?"

"Mrs. Townsend, if you'll step outside for a moment, we'll let Raeanne rest, and I'll discuss her prognosis with you."

Reluctant to leave Rae, Janelle caressed her

cheek again. "I'll be right outside the curtain. If you need me, you call real loud for me. Can you do that?"

Rae nodded slowly. "You'll come back, won't you?"

"Of course I will. As soon as I finish talking with the doctor."

When she stepped out of the cubicle, she realized Adam had left. Probably to go back to Harley, who had looked almost as upset as Adam. In a way, she wished he had stayed to hear what the doctor had to say. But he had his own daughter to worry about. Rae was her responsibility, not his.

"Doctor…" Her mind went blank. "I'm sorry, I've forgotten your name." He had a boyish face and blond hair that swept over his forehead, making him appear much too young to be an experienced physician.

"Jason Johansen. Let me assure you, your daughter is going to be just fine. She may have had a minor concussion from the hit on her head. She swallowed some lake water, but Adam reported that she spit it all out. All in all, with the few stitches I put in to close the wound, her recovery should be complete in a matter of days."

Janelle felt the tension drain from her shoulders. He might appear young, but his reassuring words and caring bedside manner gave her confidence that he knew what he was talking about. "Thank you, Doctor Johansen. I'm so sorry it was difficult to reach me."

He waved off her apology. "Raeanne will probably experience a headache for a couple of days. Just give her some Children's Tylenol. You should also check her pupils every hour or two for the next twelve hours to see that they're the same size."

"Of course."

"Other than that, I'd keep her quiet for a day or two, let her rest."

"I will. I promise." And Janelle vowed she wouldn't go running off house hunting anytime soon. "Will she have a scar?"

He lifted his lips in a half smile. "Not if I did a good job stitching her up. Her injury is right at the hairline, so worst case she can cover it with bangs. But I think she'll be fine."

"Again, I can only thank you for taking care of my little girl."

"My pleasure. You go sit with her while I work up her discharge papers. I recommend you take her to your family physician in a week or so for a follow-up."

She'd be happy to do that, if she had a family doctor here in Bear Lake. A chore that had just moved up on her priority list.

Janelle pulled up a chair next to Raeanne. "How are you feeling?"

"Can we go home now?"

"In a minute. The doctor is filling out some paperwork, then we can go. Can you tell me what happened? How did you fall into the lake?" Amazingly, the shock of the accident had brought back Raeanne's speech. She was even talking in full sentences. *The Lord works in strange and wondrous ways.*

Tears welled in Raeanne's sweet brown eyes. "I was playing with Kitty Cat and I took her outside. I thought she'd want to look at the lake. And then…" Her chin trembled. "I carried her onto the boat. She didn't like that."

"What did she do?"

"She jumped back onto the dock. I tried to catch her, Mommy."

Janelle brushed a tear from Rae's cheek. "And that's when you fell and hit your head."

"I'm sorry."

"It's all right, sweetie." Janelle lifted Raeanne from the gurney into her lap and held her close. "You're going to be fine. You'll see."

"But what about Kitty Cat? She'll be scared all by herself, and she'll get lost again."

"I'm sure she won't go far." Janelle was far more worried that some forest creature would attack the young kitten and she wouldn't be able to run away fast enough. "When we get home, I bet she'll be waiting on the deck ready for her dinner." At least she prayed that that would be the case. She'd hate for Raeanne to carry the burden of losing her beloved Kitty Cat.

In the waiting area, Adam sat with his arm around Hailey's shoulders, trying to comfort her. And trying to calm the knot of guilt that had settled in his stomach. The fear that Rae might have been more seriously injured.

"But what if Janelle's really mad at me?" Hailey's eyes were puffy and she'd used up a bunch of tissues blowing her nose. "I shouldn't have let Rae climb up on the boat."

Adam tucked a strand of her stringy, damp hair behind her ear. "Maybe not, but after Rae fell you did exactly the right thing. You jumped in and pulled her out. I think what you did was brave and smart." The real problem was that his mind had been drifting. He hadn't kept a close enough eye on the girls and should have known better.

She sniffed. "I wish there was something I could do to make Rae feel better."

"Well, now, let me think." He leaned back in the chair, wondering himself if Janelle would be mad at them both and how he could fix that. He prayed she wouldn't be angry enough to up and leave right away just to get out of his house. The fact was, he'd kind of forgotten how quickly a five-year-old could wander out of sight and get into trouble even with him close by. He'd gotten used to Hailey's unusual maturity, a result of losing her mother at such a young age.

"Daddy, I know what we can do." She eased out of the chair. "There's a gift shop over there. Maybe we can find something that will make Rae feel better."

He glanced over his shoulder. "Good idea. Let me roll up your pant legs so you don't trip over them and crack your own skull." The scrubs the nurse had given Hailey to change into from her wet clothes might be a size small for a woman, but the pant legs were six inches too long for Hailey. The shirt didn't fit much better. She looked like a little girl playing dress-up doctor.

Grabbing the bag of wet clothes, Adam followed her.

As hospital gift shops went, this one was pretty small. There were paperback books, games and puzzles, magazines, child-size T-shirts and stuffed animals.

Hailey immediately arrowed in on the stuffed animals. "Look, Daddy, there's a fuzzy teddy bear wearing a T-shirt that says Bear Lake, MT. Isn't that cute?"

"Yeah, Rae might like that." He checked the price tag and figured he could handle that. "Go ahead and get it."

She lifted the bear off the table and hugged it to her chest. "What are you going to get Janelle?"

His head snapped down to meet his daughter's gaze. "Why would I get Janelle a present?"

"Because you feel guilty that Rae was hurt and want to say you're sorry."

"I don't feel—" Yeah, he did feel guilty. But what kind of a gift would make up for not watching Raeanne carefully enough?

"She likes to read. I could help you pick out a book for her."

He eyed his daughter. Had she offered to pick out the book because she knew he couldn't read? A trickle of unease skittered down his spine.

"No, a book's too boring." He wandered around the small shop. The volunteer behind the counter, an older woman in a blue jacket, smiled at him.

"If you're looking for something special, we have some nice jewelry pieces. Everything's made by local craftsmen. I personally like the pendants with the blue Montana sapphire gemstones. They're beautiful, and buying them makes me feel proud of Montana. Plus it helps our local artists."

He glanced at the display case next to the counter. He supposed they were very pretty, but jewelry seemed too personal somehow. Assuming he could even figure out what kind of jewelry Janelle would like.

Hailey joined him at the display case. "Those

are nice, Daddy. I bet Janelle would like that silver rose with a sapphire in the middle." She turned to the volunteer. "Don't you think that would make a good gift for a lady?"

"I do, indeed."

A sound in the waiting area distracted Adam. He turned to see what was happening and saw Raeanne being pushed in a wheelchair by an elderly gentleman in a blue volunteer jacket, Janelle walking beside him.

"Give me the bear, Hailey. You go tell Janelle I'll be right out. It'll just take me a minute to buy this."

While Hailey dashed out, he put the bear on the counter and pulled out his wallet.

"What did you decide about the pendant?"

He shot another look at the necklace, then glanced into the waiting room. Janelle still looked pale, her brow furrowed with worry. And he was the one who had messed up not watching Rae carefully enough.

Janelle deserved something special. Something classy. Something as beautiful as she was that said that he was sorry.

He turned back to the volunteer. "I'll take it."

"Would you like them gift wrapped?"

"Um, no, that's okay." He looked toward the lobby. "I'm in kind of a hurry."

She put the necklace into a little gift box anyway.

He strummed his fingers on the countertop while she wrote up the sale. As soon as he'd signed for the credit charge, he gave the woman a smile, took the bag she'd put the bear and necklace in and hurried out of the shop.

Hailey met him halfway. "Can I give Rae her teddy bear?"

"Sure."

She snatched the gift from the bag and jogged back to Rae's side.

Adam followed more slowly. Would Janelle think he was crazy giving her the pendant? Maybe he was crossing a line she wouldn't want crossed. Maybe he'd embarrass her with a personal gift like the necklace. If she didn't like it, he could always return it to the gift shop for a refund.

The girls and Janelle were oohing and aahing over the silly teddy bear. He stood apart, not knowing what to do. Except for his mother, he hadn't given a woman a present of any kind since Lisa. His mouth went dry. What was he going to say?

She looked up at him. "I'm afraid we're going to have to ask you for a ride home. I left my car at Sharon's office. She's going to have someone drive it to your place."

He licked his lips. "No problem. My truck's parked right out front."

"Young man," the volunteer said, "why don't

you go get your truck and bring it up to the door? That way these young ladies won't have to walk so far."

"Sure, I can do that." He extended the jewelry box to Janelle. "This is for you. It's, uh, my way of saying I'm sorry." His cheeks heated as if he'd gotten a bad windburn out on his boat.

"You're sorry?" She took the box. "Why are you—"

"I'll go get the truck." He trotted out the door, anxious to get out of there. He didn't want to see her reaction. She might hate the necklace. Or think he was some kind of a geek for giving it to her.

And the fact was, the one thing she wanted from him wasn't jewelry. She wanted him to learn to read. She wanted to change him.

He wasn't sure he had the courage to try...and risk failure again.

Janelle stood rooted in place, watching him leave the lobby in a rush. Whatever was going on? They weren't in that big a hurry to leave.

"You should open the box, Janelle," Hailey said. "I think you'll like it."

Raeanne looked up at her expectantly. "Did Adam give you a teddy bear, too, to make you feel better?"

"I don't think so." The box wasn't big enough for that. Carefully she lifted the lid. She drew in a quick breath. "Oh, my..." A delicate silver rose on a chain was nestled on a bed of cotton. In the center of the rose, a blue stone sparkled. Her heartbeat quickened.

Hailey peered into the box. "That's a Montana sapphire. The lady said the pendant was made by a local craftsman."

"It's beautiful. But Adam shouldn't be giving me—"

"Let me see, Mommy."

She held the box lower.

"Excuse me, ma'am. I think your husband has brought the truck around now."

She lifted her head to correct the gentleman's assumption and thought better of it. Her relationship with Adam was far too complicated to explain to a stranger, particularly since he'd just given her a lovely gift for no reason at all.

"All right, let's go, girls. Hang on to your bag of clothes and your teddy bear, Rae."

She put the lid back on the gift box and closed it tightly in her hand. It felt warm there, as though the residual heat of Adam's hand clung to the box.

As she walked toward the exit, that same heat slid up her neck to warm her cheeks. What did his gift mean? It felt too personal, too extravagant, for a simple "I'm sorry" kind of gift.

Down deep in her heart, she hoped it meant

more to Adam than he'd let on, but she was afraid that that was only wishful thinking.

Not wanting to be separated from Raeanne, Janelle slid into the truck's backseat with her. Hailey sat up front next to her dad.

Janelle leaned forward. "The necklace is beautiful, Adam, but there really wasn't any need for you to apologize."

He shifted into gear. "If you don't like it, I can take it back to the gift shop. No big deal."

It might not be a big deal for Adam, but it was for her. Raymond hadn't been much of a gift giver. Certainly he'd never been so spontaneous that he'd pick up a necklace on a sudden impulse. Remembering Christmas was about his limit in the giving department.

"I'll put it on when we get home." She leaned back and put her arm around Raeanne, who held the teddy bear snuggled in her arms. A very thoughtful gift on Hailey's part and Adam's.

At home, Adam parked his truck close to the house. He hopped out and opened Raeanne's door.

"Come on, Buttercup. I'll carry you inside."

"I have to look for Kitty Cat. She'll be afraid all alone."

"Let Adam carry you, sweetie. Hailey and I will find the cat while you rest a little."

"Up you come." Adam scooped Raeanne up in his arms. "It's not often I get a chance to carry a pretty little girl into my house." He winked at Hailey, who'd come around to his side of the truck.

Following Adam, Janelle reached out to give Hailey a squeeze. "Your dad's a pretty nice guy, isn't he?"

"Yeah, he is. *Most* of the time."

Janelle squelched a smile. Hailey's teenage years were fast approaching.

Inside, Adam lay Rae on the couch. Janelle found a light blanket to cover her and sat down beside her.

"How do you feel now?"

"My head still hurts." Her whiny, helpless tone sliced into Janelle's heart. Her poor baby.

"You close your eyes and rest."

Rae's lower lip poked out and tears threatened. "I want Kitty Cat."

"Look!" Hailey slid open the glass door to the deck. "She's right here waiting for us."

The kitten bounded into the house as if her tail was on fire. She leaped up onto Raeanne and began kneading her tummy. Rae giggled, scratching the kitty's head.

Janelle stood back. Kitty Cat was the best medicine possible for Raeanne. *Thank You, Lord.*

Edging away from the couch, she felt for the jewelry box in the pocket of her slacks. She glanced toward Adam, who was standing by the fireplace watching her, his arms folded across his chest. Her heart lurched. With his face so serious, what could he be thinking? Was he sorry he gave her the necklace? Or was he still feeling guilty about Raeanne?

Opening the box, she looked at the lovely rose on a delicate silver chain and then back at Adam.

"Would you do the honors?" she asked, holding out the box as she walked toward him.

His Adam's apple bounced as he took the box and lifted the necklace out. "I'm usually all thumbs when it comes to stuff like this."

His hands were large and muscular, with short, even nails, and as gentle as those of any man she'd ever known.

"I think you'll be able to manage." She turned her back to him.

After a moment's hesitation, he lifted her hair away from her neck, sending gooseflesh down her spine. The backs of his fingers brushed her nape, lingered as he worked the clasp.

"There you go." His voice deeper and more husky than usual, he stepped back.

She adjusted the rose in the hollow at the base of her throat where her pulse beat so heavily. She turned toward him. "How does it look?"

His gaze focused on the pendant, then slowly he raised his eyes to meet hers. Electricity sizzled between them as though the power of yesterday's thunderstorm still raged.

"I've been thinking." Speaking softly, he continued to keep her snared with the power of his intensity. "If you can figure out what I'm supposed to do, I'd like to try that online class you were talking about. The one that might help me read better."

Chapter Thirteen

Adam spent the following morning second-guessing himself and looking for an excuse not to take the online class. It had to have been her perfume—something light and flowery—that had taken over his mind when he lifted her hair off her neck. And then the feel of her baby-soft skin got into the act.

How could a man think straight with all of that going on?

He should have skipped the necklace. Except seeing it resting just below her throat, where everyone could see the gift *he* gave her, was enough to drive any man loony. Willing to say or do anything to keep her close.

He flexed his jaw. He'd talk her out of the whole idea. That's what he'd do.

"I don't want to sit out in the garage half the night working on my computer," he complained to Janelle, who had come into the garage office to do some work while Rae was taking a nap.

An I-know-what-you're-doing smile tilted her lips. "We can use my laptop and set it up on the dining-room table."

He shoved his hands into his overall pockets. "No way could I concentrate with the girls hanging over my shoulder. Besides, I don't want Hailey to know what I'm up to." Nor did he want to be forced to admit he had dyslexia.

Her nicely arched brows lifted, her eyes challenging his excuses. "You can do the program after the girls have gone to bed."

Despite his best efforts, Janelle countered every excuse he offered. She was a whole lot smarter and less susceptible to his boyish charm than the teachers he'd conned in school to get himself out of a jam.

He must be losing his touch.

That evening after the girls were in bed, Janelle pulled a chair around so she could sit next to Adam at the dining table and see the computer screen.

"I talked to the program coordinator this afternoon," she said. "You're all set to go. To start, you simply have to double-click the icon on the left."

He stared at the screen. The tightness of his shoulders, the grim set to his jaw, screamed that he didn't want to do this. She could almost hear him loudly complain, *"I'd rather eat tacks."*

Poor guy.

A deep inhale raised his chest, apparently giving him enough courage to click the icon. The screen filled and a voice welcomed him to Fast-Track Reading, then it asked that he click on lesson one.

"How many lessons are there?" he asked.

"I don't know. The description said it usually takes three to four months to complete the course."

"You're kidding!" He glared at her and his voice rose. "I'm not going to sit here every night for four months fussing with some reading program."

"It's only for a half hour per night and only five nights a week. Unless you want to do more."

"Yeah, right!" He barked a humorless laugh. "As if I'd want to do more just for the fun of it."

Janelle had no doubt his attitude and anger were born of many years of frustration and repeated failure. Fear kept him rooted in his old habits, finding work-arounds to disguise his limitations or blustering his way through when discovery was threatened.

"Adam, listen to me." She rested her hand on his forearm. "You're a successful businessman. Everyone in town respects and loves you. You're a great dad. You've conquered every challenge that you've faced and overcome all the odds. You're a genius when it comes to fixing cars. Now is the time to face this challenge—your dyslexia."

Adam speared his fingers through his hair. All the fight went out of him, and he nodded. He'd told her he'd try the computer lessons. He couldn't back out now. "Okay, what do I do next?"

She gave his arm an encouraging squeeze. "Click on lesson one."

The screen filled with colorful animated characters waving back at them. Music swelled. A dapper-looking owl stepped forward. "Hi there. I'm Ollie the Owl, and I'm going to help you navigate Fast-Track Reading. You'll be surprised how soon you'll learn to read faster and understand more."

Shocked and humiliated, Adam shoved back his chair and stood. "It's a cartoon program! For kids! You can turn the thing off. I'm not going to make a fool of myself with some fake barn owl."

Closing her eyes, Janelle cringed. "I'm sorry."

"Daddy?"

Simultaneously, they both turned toward Hailey, wide-eyed and standing at the entrance to the living room in her nightgown.

"I heard you yelling. Is something wrong?"

"Nothing's wrong." He reached behind him to close the laptop. This was his worst nightmare, that Hailey would find out about his dyslexia. "You go on back to bed now. Everything's fine."

"Tell her the truth, Adam," Janelle whispered.

He couldn't!

"Were you and Janelle having a fight?"

"No, of course not." He got the lid closed. His palms were damp, his mouth dry. "You want me to come tuck you in again?"

"She loves you, Adam. She'll be so proud of what you're trying to do. Tell her." Janelle's voice was ripping him apart.

"No, it's okay." Hailey's gaze shifted between them. "Can I get a drink of water?"

"Sure, Peanut. Help yourself."

Still keeping an eye on him, she walked barefoot into the kitchen, got down a glass from the cupboard and filled it with water. What was she thinking? Was the water an excuse to hang around, find out what he'd been hiding all these years?

"So if you aren't mad at Janelle, why were you yelling?" A good question from a kid who wore a troubled expression.

Problem was, Adam didn't have a good answer.

"It's nothing," Adam repeated. "I was just mad at myself, that's all."

"Why?"

As hard as he tried, he still couldn't come up with a ready answer. He shifted his weight from one foot to the other. A hangnail on his thumb drew his interest. He couldn't meet her eyes.

"See, here's the thing," he began with a shrug he tried to make casual. "I'm not a real good reader.

Janelle found this program online that might help me to speed up my reading. It's kind of a dorky thing for kids, and I got—"

"You're going to learn to read? Really?" A big smile brightened Hailey's face.

"Well, you know, I can read," he backpedaled. "This is just a way to read faster. I'm not even sure I'm going to try it."

Hailey left her glass of water on the counter and ran to Adam, hugging him tightly. "This is great, Dad. I didn't know there was a way to fix it so you could read. Now you'll be able to read all the books you want to and help me with my homework and everything."

He met Janelle's gaze over the top of Hailey's head.

Tell her the truth, she silently mouthed.

He pursed his lips and squeezed his eyes closed. It would kill him to have his daughter think he was stupid. But could he keep lying to her, making excuses? Hiding the truth? A truth it seemed she'd already figured out.

"Hailey, sweetheart, there's something I need to tell you." He sat down in the chair and held her hands. "See, the truth is, I really can't read. I've never been able to, not very well, anyway. I've got something called dyslexia."

She stood there silent for a moment while he held his breath waiting for her reaction. "It's no big deal, Dad. I've known forever that you couldn't really read. I'm just glad Janelle's helping you."

He shook his head. "You're not ashamed of me?"

"Why would I be ashamed of you? You're the best dad in the whole world. Everybody knows that." She hugged him again. "I gotta get back to bed. Don't study too hard."

With that, she dashed back down the hallway to her bedroom, leaving Adam totally nonplused.

He turned to Janelle, who was smiling like a Cheshire cat. *Smart aleck!* He wanted to wipe that smile off her face. Instead he found his own lips lifting into a grin.

"She said it's no big deal." He felt light-headed, kind of floating, as if a big weight had been lifted from his shoulders.

Tears glistened in Janelle's eyes. Good tears, he thought. Tears of approval. Maybe even a little more than approval.

"So, does that mean you want to get started on lesson one?"

Slowly, he lifted the laptop lid. Gut-wrenching fear tangled with hope. Sweat dampened his palms. Yeah, he'd try again. Maybe he'd get it right this time.

Sharon called the following morning to check on Raeanne. She wanted to meet for coffee and discuss the Jackson house.

Janelle declined. "I'm sorry, Sharon. For the next day or two I'm going to stick close to home, keep an eye on Raeanne." Plus she needed to recover from her attack of guilt that she'd been nearly unreachable when her daughter needed her.

"How would it be if I come to you? You can make the coffee and I'll bring doughnuts for all of us, including Adam and the girls."

That offer was hard to turn down. Among other things, the beginning of school was fast approaching. Janelle wanted to get Raeanne enrolled, but until she settled on a house she didn't have a permanent address to give to the administration. Giving Adam's address would invite too many questions.

It wasn't so much that she was concerned about what others might think about their relationship. In fact, it was the opposite. She had no idea what their relationship was. And that was something she didn't want to push.

She'd chalked up one less-than-successful marriage in part because she had pushed Raymond for a commitment long before he was ready. She'd been young and filled with the fantasy of marriage. She'd gone right from living with her mother to being Raymond's wife.

She needed to prove her own independence before stepping into a new relationship. That's what the counselor in Seattle had said.

So Janelle agreed to Sharon's idea, and the Realtor showed up at the house right at 10:30 with a bakery box of doughnuts in her arms.

"I stopped in the garage to give Adam and Vern first choice." She placed the box on the kitchen table and opened the lid. "Vern was on the chocolate donut like ants at a picnic. Adam took a glazed one, but I bought two of everything so you can have your choice."

Both girls came running. Kitty Cat raced along behind them as though she was due for a treat, too.

"Can we have any one we want?" Hailey asked.

"You certainly may." Sharon moved the box to provide easy access.

In a nanosecond, Hailey made chocolate her choice.

Raeanne, still frequently quiet with strangers, carefully plucked a jelly-filled doughnut from the box.

Mentally, Janelle pictured the sugar high the girls were about to experience and laughed. Keeping Raeanne quiet the rest of the day might be a challenge. What a blessed problem.

Letting the girls eat in the kitchen, Janelle took the pot of coffee, cups, plates and napkins to the dining table, where she sat down with Sharon.

After she poured the coffee, Janelle took a bite of the extra-glazed donut and nearly moaned with pleasure. "I have the feeling you're trying to wear down my resistance with a sugar overdose."

Sharon laughed. "That wasn't my plan. But if it works, that's fine by me." She opened the Jackson house file and spread out the photos. "I don't think you had a chance to see all of the extras at the house yesterday, since we had to rush away. We could go back and take another walk through, if you'd like."

"No, I don't think I need to do that. It's a beautiful place, but the bottom line is I still don't think I can afford that house. It's really too big for just the two of us anyway."

Sharon stirred some milk into her coffee and took a sip. "I think they'll come down in their price quite a bit. We could make an offer and see what they say." She named an amount that was twenty thousand dollars less than the listing price.

"That almost sounds unfair to the Jacksons. They're lovely people."

"People who are eager to move to be nearer their grandchildren."

Janelle still didn't feel right about buying the house. Even the lower price was a bit of a stretch. Until she found some regular employment, she didn't know what her income would be. It would be awful to move into the house and then have to sell it, uprooting Raeanne again.

Apparently, Sharon sensed her resistance. "Tell

you what, I brought along some forms from the bank. You can get a preapproval for a loan, and then you'll know exactly how much your mortgage payments will be. The interest rates right now are so low, you'd be amazed how little you'll have to pay." She slid the papers toward Janelle.

Having finished their doughnuts, the girls were eager to go out and play.

"You may go outside, but stay where I can see you." Janelle hooked her hand around Raeanne's head and pulled her closer for a kiss on the forehead. "No climbing into Adam's boat, okay? And no running around. I don't want you falling down."

"Okay," she responded in her quiet voice.

After the girls left, Sharon resumed the conversation. "Even if you decide not to buy the Jackson place, you'll still have the preapproved loan available to buy another house. It's a win-win situation. From what you've told me, I know your credit must be good."

Reasonably confident her credit was okay, she scanned the forms. Income, assets, debts and credit-card information. Not too hard to complete.

Feeling pressured by both her current living situation and Sharon's eager sales pitch, she nodded. "I just have to fill out the forms and take them to the bank here in town?"

"That's it. Paul Muskie is the bank president. He'll take good care of you if he's in. The answer will come back in a few days, then you'll know just where you stand."

Kitty Cat jumped into Janelle's lap and tried to get to the doughnut box. Janelle held her firmly, petting her and skinning her ears back flat against her head.

Determining just how large a loan she could get and what the payments would be seemed a reasonable step to take. It didn't commit her to any particular house. Maybe she could purchase something less expensive than the Jackson place and make smaller payments.

"I'll fill out the forms this afternoon and take them to the bank tomorrow," she promised.

Before Sharon left, she gave Janelle a recommendation for a pediatrician in town. Janelle planned to call right away to set up an appointment for Raeanne. She seemed fine after her accident, but Janelle wanted to make sure. Moving across the country involved a lot of changes. She needed to get her act together, reestablish the bits and pieces of her life. She couldn't rely on Adam forever.

Adam cleaned up in the garage before he came in for dinner. He'd had a crank shaft to replace, the old one caked with dirt and grease from about a million years of sitting in a vacant lot beside the owner's house. The guy was finally getting it ready to sell.

As he walked up to the front door of the house, he eyed the wreath of dried flowers and pinecones, all tied with a blue ribbon, that Janelle had hung there. Nice touch. Made the place look homey. As if a woman lived here.

Except Sharon's visit that morning had reminded him that Janelle might not be living here much longer. She was intent on buying a house. Which was okay, he told himself. That had been her plan when she arrived in town.

That thought made him realize that he'd miss her more than he'd be willing to admit to her or anyone else. But he and Hailey had been on their own for three years. No harm done when it went back to being just the two of them. They'd get along fine. They had up until Janelle and her daughter had entered their lives, hadn't they?

Or was that wishful thinking?

Inside, he found the girls sitting in the middle of the living room with bits of cardboard, Scotch tape and scissors scattered all around. A couple of old shoe boxes were stacked on top of each other.

"What are you girls up to?"

"Janelle's helping us to make a house for Rae's miniature wooden dolls." She held up a two-inch doll wearing what looked like a calico dress.

"After we get the house made, we can make furniture—beds and tables and stuff."

"Sounds very creative." Something he'd never have thought to suggest.

He strolled into the kitchen, where Janelle was fixing a salad. "Need any help?"

"No, I'm good. A chicken-and-noodle casserole is in the oven. It'll will be done in about ten minutes."

"Great. I'm starved."

She shot him a grin. "Hard day at the office?"

"Hard day at the garage with me on my back getting oil and gunk dripped on my face."

She wrinkled her nose. "Sounds like a lot of fun."

"Not really." He leaned back against the counter to watch her slice tomatoes. "So have you and Sharon decided on a house for you to buy?"

"Not really. I am going to the bank tomorrow to submit papers so I can get a preapproved loan. That was Sharon's idea. I'll know then how much I can afford to buy."

"Sounds reasonable." He plucked a crouton from the bag on the counter. It also sounded as if she was getting one step closer to making a decision, which would lead to her moving out of the cottage.

He almost choked on that thought and had to grab a glass of water to swallow the dry crouton past the tightness of his throat.

Later, after they'd had dinner and the girls were in bed, he sat down with Janelle's laptop at the dining-room table. He furrowed his brow in determination. No matter how hard the lesson was, or how frustrating, he was going to get through it and move on to the next one.

He turned the sound down low so the stupid owl wouldn't shout the lesson for the whole house to hear.

This time he wasn't going to fail. His gut told him there was more at stake than just his ability to read an IRS form.

Chapter Fourteen

Janelle decided to take the girls with her to the bank and treat them to lunch at the diner after her business was concluded. They'd both been very good about staying close to home since Raeanne's accident and deserved a reward.

The bank had a definite Rocky Mountain feel, with paintings of towering, snow-clad peaks, endless forests and pristine lakes mounted on knotty pine walls. The quiet, unhurried pace and low hum of conversation reminded Janelle of a meadow with a nearby bubbling brook spilling over water-rounded stones.

Paul Muskie, the bank president, wasn't in, so the teller referred Janelle to the manager, Andrew Muskie, the president's son.

The younger Muskie's desk sat off to the side away from the tellers. As Janelle approached, she was struck by the young man's relative youth, perhaps in his early thirties. It seemed promotion came fast in this family-run organization.

Despite his apparent youth, he wore the uniform of a serious banker—a dark, well-tailored suit, white shirt and an uninspired tie.

"Mr. Muskie?"

He lifted his head to reveal blue eyes that danced with intelligence and welcome. He came to his feet, sparing a quick look at the two girls. His smile creased his cheek.

"Yes. How can I help you?"

She first introduced herself, then the girls.

He immediately recognized Adam's daughter. "How's it going, Hailey?"

"Fine, I guess. Janelle's going to take us to lunch."

"Lucky you. Say hello to your dad for me." He turned back to Janelle.

"I've been house hunting with Sharon Brevik. She suggested I get a preapproved loan so I'll know what my payments might be." She handed him the completed forms.

"Excellent. Please sit down." He pulled over an extra chair from a nearby desk so they could all be seated. The girls each claimed a chair and sat primly with their hands in their laps. Raeanne's chair was so large that when she sat all the way back, her feet stuck out in front of her. Janelle sat back, crossed her legs and adjusted the hem of her skirt.

"So you're planning to settle here in the area?" Andrew asked.

"That's the plan. Assuming the housing situation works out."

"Excellent," he repeated. "You and your husband will find Bear Lake a great place to raise children."

Her fingertips brushed the silver-and-sapphire necklace at her throat, remembering the last time someone had referred to her husband. "I'm a widow."

"Oh." His expression immediately sobered. "I'm sorry for your loss."

She nodded in acknowledgment. No need for her to go into details.

He skimmed the forms quickly. "I see you're working for Adam."

"Part-time as a bookkeeper. After I settle in I hope to find more work."

A shallow V formed between his brows.

She tensed, uncrossed her legs and leaned forward. "Is that a problem?" She couldn't imagine having trouble getting a loan, considering the amount of cash she was willing to put down on a house.

"Our loan officer is at our branch in Kalispell. He's the one who makes the decisions about loans and so on. It's above my pay grade, I'm afraid." His smile looked forced, his dimple failing to appear. "I'm confident he'll be able to work something out for you."

Suddenly she was far less confident of getting a loan than when she had walked in the door.

"When do you suppose I might hear back?"

"This being Wednesday, I should think we'd hear by Friday, Monday at the latest."

"Then I'll look forward to hearing from you, Mr. Muskie." She stood and shook hands with him, but behind her smile she hid a frown. The meeting hadn't gone nearly as well as she had expected or hoped.

Adam closed up shop early that afternoon. Word around town was that there was a late stonefly hatch in Arrowhead Cove. The flying insects were a gourmet treat for fish, and the rainbow trout were going crazy.

He found the girls down by the lake building a fort out of driftwood. "Hey, ladies. Who wants to go fishing?"

Hailey immediately jumped to her feet. "I do! I do!"

Janelle, who had brought a beach chair down to the dock and was reading, lowered her dark glasses. "Can you just close up shop in the middle of the day?"

"Sure. That's the advantage of owning your own business." He grabbed Hailey, lifting her in the air and setting her on her feet again. "Go put on some long pants. It may cool off before we get home. You, too, Rae, if you want to come along. When we get back we'll have a fire right here on the beach and cook our fish over the coals."

Rae looked to her mother for approval.

"Neither of us have ever been fishing," Janelle said. "Much less cooked fish over an open fire."

"Then it's a great time to learn. The flies are hatching in Arrowhead Cove and the fish are jumping."

"Flies? Jumping fish?" Shaking her head, Janelle stood. "Aren't we supposed to have a license to fish?"

"The girls are good without a license. We'll get you one later. I know the Fish and Wildlife guy, so no problem. Now, time's a'wasting."

At Janelle's obvious reluctance, Adam grinned. "You aren't allowed to be a permanent resident of Montana without knowing how to fish. I'm sure that's written someplace in the state constitution."

She folded up her chair. "Based on my experience at the bank this morning, I may not get a loan big enough to become a permanent resident."

He did a mental double-take at that news. Why on earth wouldn't Muskie grant her a loan?

"Go get changed and bag up some snacks and

drinks for us," he said. "I'll get our gear and we'll talk about that once we're under way."

From his stash of fishing gear in the shed at the far side of the house, he retrieved several spinning outfits and fly-fishing poles. He got enough for himself and Janelle, if she wanted to try that. Along with his tackle box, he carried all the gear to the boat. He made a second trip to retrieve the life vests and a pair of oars, just in case.

By the time he got everything safely stowed in the boat and checked that he had enough gasoline, Janelle and the girls had returned wearing warmer clothes and carrying jackets.

"Okay, everybody hang tight. We're going across the lake." Hailey loosened the mooring lines for him and then jumped back in the boat. Slowly he eased the boat away from the dock. Janelle sat next to him up front with the girls settled in the open cockpit.

Janelle tugged her baseball cap down firmly on her head. "I feel like this is senior ditch day in high school."

He shot her a grin. "Everyone needs to take a break sometime." He accelerated and the boat rode up higher on the water.

"How do you know the fish are jumping in this cove you're taking us to?" she asked, holding her cap in place. She'd pulled her hair back into a ponytail and stuck it through the opening in the back of the cap. The ponytail swished back and forth in sync with the rocking boat like a flag signaling a friendly greeting.

"There's sort of an informal telephone tree among the locals. One guy spots the hatch and texts his buddy. The word spreads pretty fast."

"You do texting?"

He grinned. "*Fish* isn't that hard a word to read."

"But you don't share the news with the tourists."

"Not if we can help it."

She laughed. "Then I guess I'm lucky I know a local."

"You better believe it, kiddo." He steered a little to starboard. He spotted one other boat en route to the cove. Looked like old Ron Taylor, a local plumber, in his aging cruiser. The guy spent more time fishing than he did fixing broken pipes and replacing hot-water tanks. If the fishing was good, you could forget about seeing him.

"So what happened at the bank this morning?" he asked over the sound of the wind and the engine noise.

"I turned in my papers for the preapproved loan. Andrew Muskie acted as though my not having a regular job might be a problem."

"You told him you planned to work part-time, didn't you?"

"Yes. He didn't seem impressed."

Adam scowled. While he wasn't eager for Janelle

to move out of the cottage, he didn't like the idea of her being turned down for a loan, either. "Maybe I can talk to Paul, Andrew's dad. Kind of smooth a path for you." It was the least he could do, since Janelle had been the one to get him off the hook with the IRS. That ought to carry some weight with Paul.

"Anything you can do to help, I'd appreciate. I'm worried about getting settled before school starts."

"I'll give him a call tomorrow." He eased back on the power as they approached the cove. He watched a fish rise. Ripples circled out from where the fish had surfaced to snatch a fly from the air.

He grinned. *Here comes dinner!*

Janelle looked around the cove in awe. Shaped exactly like an arrowhead, a stream entered the lake at the tip of the arrow.

Fir trees grew all the way to the shoreline. The trees grew so close together, no sign of human encroachment appeared possible. A huge bird's nest sat perched in the top of one tree. As she watched, a giant white bird with a fish held in its claws circled the nest and then landed with the grace of a ballerina.

"Looks like the local osprey are on our text-messaging service, too." Adam switched off the motor, letting the boat drift in the quiet cove.

"She's beautiful."

"Just as long as she leaves a few fish for us." He pulled the fishing poles from under the seats in the cockpit.

Janelle didn't have a clue what he was doing, but she watched with interest as he deftly put the poles together and strung the fishing line through the eyelets. He tied hooks at the end of the lines, added a couple of orange salmon eggs and slid a red plastic ball Adam had called a bobber in place. The man had good hands, she'd give him that.

Another boat putted into the cove and cut the motor. Adam waved to the fisherman, who tipped his cap in response.

"There you go, Hailey." He handed his daughter one of the poles. "See if you can cast your line over there, as close to the big rock as you can get it."

With considerable expertise, at least in Janelle's eyes, Hailey tossed the line exactly where Adam had instructed.

"Good job," she said.

"Hailey's been fishing since she was about four years old," Adam told her with obvious pride in his voice. "Okay, Buttercup, let me see if we can get you a great big fish for dinner."

Standing behind Rae, he put her hands in place, covered them with his own and then cast the line out over the stern of the boat.

"All right. Now, you hang on to that fishing pole

real tight and watch that little red bobber out there. If it jiggles, you pull real hard."

Wide-eyed and intent on her responsibility, she nodded.

"Now then, Ms. Townsend. Spinning gear or a fly rod?"

"I think we novices ought to stick with spinning gear."

"You got it." He put together another rig and showed her how to hold the pole and cast, letting go of the line as it shot out. "Give it a try," he ordered.

Totally lacking any confidence she could cast properly, must less catch anything, she reared back and tossed the line toward the water.

Unfortunately, she hadn't let go of the line as instructed. Instead, the lead section of the line with the bobber, hook and salmon eggs spun around the pole, the salmon eggs flying off in the process, plopping into the water about five feet from the boat.

Adam coughed and choked, trying to prevent the laugh that sparkled in his eyes.

Her own laughter bubbled up. "Oopsy. Looks like I could use another lesson."

"Daddy! I caught one."

Janelle turned to see Hailey reeling in her line. Adam stepped quickly to her side. "Keep your line taut. Thatta girl. When he gets close, he'll see the boat and make a run for it. Hold on tight."

He grabbed a long-handled net and leaned over the side of the boat. Hailey's line bent over with the weight and pull of the fish.

"He's a monster, Daddy. I know he is."

"A record breaker. Here we go." He scooped up the fish and dropped it into the cockpit. "Good job! Looks like at least fourteen inches long. Your personal best, squirt."

A rainbow stripe of color glistened on the side of the wet fish.

Before Adam could get the flopping fish off the hook, Raeanne announced, "My bobber jiggled."

"Hey, all right!"

He went to help her bring in the fish, but it had gotten off the hook, along with the bait. So he reeled it in to put more eggs on her hook and then cast the line out again.

"Watch it good this time. When it bobs, yank real hard."

He returned to the fish Hailey had caught, took care of it and checked her line.

Coming back to Janelle, he untangled her line and set the bait. "Okay, let's try this again."

"At the rate we're going, you're not going to have time to do any fishing yourself," she pointed out.

"I just have to get everyone organized." He

stood with his arms around her, guiding her hands. She swung the pole back and then started the forward motion, determined to get it right this time.

"Ouch! Ow! Stop!"

"What's wrong?" She turned quickly. The pole slipped from her grasp.

"Grab the—"

The pole splashed into the water.

"Daddy, what's wrong?"

"My bobber jiggled again!"

He clamped his hand over his shoulder. "The hook. It caught me in the shoulder. Hailey, help Rae." He gritted his teeth.

"Let me see." He turned so Janelle could take a look. Janelle gasped. "How in the world—" The hook had gone through his shirt right into his flesh. Her stomach clenched.

"See if you can haul the pole back up before we lose it."

"I need to get that hook out of you."

"It'll wait."

"Rae caught a fish! It's a rainbow."

"Get the net."

Torn between helping Adam, seeing her grinning daughter catch her first fish or retrieving the fishing pole, Janelle opted to do as she'd been told. The boat didn't ride very high out of the water. She leaned over the side to snare the line to pull up the pole. Just as she gripped it, the boat rocked in the wake of a passing boat. She lost her balance. And fell into the lake. Headfirst.

The icy-cold water stunned her. She gasped, swallowing a mouthful of the lake water before she popped to the surface. She shook the water from her eyes and coughed.

Adam leaned over the side toward her. "You okay?"

"The water's really, really cold."

"Yeah, I know. Grab my hand and I'll pull you up."

"Oh, no, Rae's fish got away," Hailey cried.

With amazing arm strength, Adam lifted Janelle out of the water and helped her into the boat. He held her for a moment, steadying her. Looking into her eyes, he brushed a wet strand of hair away from her face. He warmed her cheek with his palm.

"You know what? I think I just caught the best-looking fish in the lake."

As the warmth of his look and words heated her from the inside out, she smiled up at him. Her heart fluttered. "Seems to me I hooked a pretty handsome fish myself."

"Dad, what happened to Janelle?" Hailey asked, finally noticing what was going on in the bow of the boat.

Adam held Janelle a moment longer before releasing her. "She decided to take a swim. Can you bring me my tackle box and the first-aid kit?"

Looking puzzled, Hailey brought him what he'd asked for. He cut the line to the pole Janelle had dropped in the water, making it a total loss, then she used a pair of long-nose pliers to work the hook out of his shoulder.

"I'm so sorry," she whispered.

"Don't worry about it. This has to be the most memorable fishing trip I've ever taken."

She began to shiver as she dabbed some anti-biotic cream from his first-aid kit on his wound and covered it with a bandage.

Adam put away the fishing gear, and they headed home. As he'd said, Janelle's first fishing adventure was one she wouldn't soon forget. Nor would her heart.

Adam convinced Hailey to freeze her fish until they had enough to feed everyone.

While Janelle was taking a shower to warm up, he found a couple of cans of chili con carne in the cupboard and dumped them in a pan to heat. With a little grated cheese on top, that would do for dinner.

Once they'd all been seated at the table and said grace, Rae looked him in the eye, her expression grave.

"I lost my fish," she said.

"Yeah, I know. That happens sometimes." When her head dipped in defeat, he lifted her chin. "I promise we'll go back one day soon to catch him again."

"We will?"

He leaned over to kiss her on the top of her head. "You bet, Buttercup. He won't get away next time."

As he resumed eating his chili, he smiled to himself. As outgoing as Hailey was, Raeanne was the complete opposite, yet he knew he could love them both equally. If he were given the chance.

They'd almost finished eating when there was a knock on the door.

Frowning, and wondering who'd be at his door this time of night, Adam shoved back his chair. "I'll get it."

He found three of his Rotary friends standing on the front porch.

"Uh-oh. Looks like I'm outnumbered." He opened the door wider. "Come on in. We're just finishing up dinner."

As he started to introduce his friends, he noticed Janelle had already scooped up the dirty bowls and put them in the sink. His friends appeared more than a little interested to find a strange woman making herself at home in his house.

"Guys, I'd like you to meet Janelle Townsend and her daughter, Raeanne. I think you all know

Hailey." He put his hand on Charlie's shoulder. "This is Charlie Brooks, Owen Marcus and Ed Downey. They're all Rotary Club members, probably here to kidnap me as some kind of a fundraising stunt."

Charlie laughed. "Not this time, buddy."

"I'm glad to meet you," Janelle said. "I'm sorry I can't offer you anything for dinner, but I can put a pot of coffee on and there are some cookies."

"No, we're fine," Ed said. "Very sorry we interrupted your dinner, ma'am. We came by to talk to Adam about Rotary business."

"Go right ahead." Janelle rested her hand on Rae's shoulder. "Why don't you girls go play in Hailey's room for a bit? We'll let these gentlemen take care of their business."

The girls left, and Janelle continued to clean up the dishes.

Adam ushered the men into the living room, where they all sat down. Adam crossed his ankle over his opposite knee. His gaze hopped between his friends. "What's up?"

"I guess you know," Ed began. "We're the nominating committee. We've come to recruit you."

Adam shot a look at Charlie. "Your idea?"

"We're all in agreement, Adam. You're our choice for our next president."

Adam's hand tightened on his ankle. The chili

threatened a rebellion. "You've wasted your time, fellas. The answer is no."

"Your excuse of being too busy isn't good enough," Charlie said.

"The job isn't as big and demanding as you might think." Owen had served two terms as president. He'd done a fine job, but he'd been having health problems lately.

"I don't know how else to say it. No. No, I won't serve as president." He dropped his foot to the floor. "If that's all you had on your minds…" He stood to signal the end of the conversation.

Ed came to his feet, too. "Could you at least think about it for a day or two?"

"I don't need to think about it. My answer isn't going to change."

Owen tried another approach, trying to guilt him into serving, reminding him how long he'd been a member. How everyone had to do their share. Adam remained firm. For good reason. If he couldn't read, he couldn't handle the job no matter how much he might want to.

Worse, sooner or later, they'd all realize their high-and-not-so-mighty leader was illiterate. Wouldn't that be a surprise?

He escorted them out. When he shut the door behind them, he exhaled in relief. He ran his palm along the back of his neck to ease his tension. His shame had escaped detection. This time.

"You should have told them why you don't want to be president."

His head snapped around. Janelle stood at the edge of the entryway.

"That's not going to happen."

"They'd understand if you told them the truth, Adam. Just as Hailey did. They aren't going to respect you any less when they find out you're dyslexic. You should tell them."

"I can't." He walked past her into the living room. It was one thing to have told Hailey. She had to love him; he was her father.

But his friends? They'd laugh themselves sick at his expense. A grown man unable to read a children's book, much less the minutes of the last meeting?

Lisa had been right. No way was he going to reveal the secret he'd kept so long.

Chapter Fifteen

Late Friday afternoon, Janelle's cell phone rang while she was mopping up a juice spill on the kitchen floor. A spurt of anxiety zipped through her when she read the local number. Not the Realtor. It had to be the bank.

"Hello, Ms. Townsend," a firm male voice said. "I'm Paul Muskie from Montana Federal. Our loan department has made a decision on your loan application."

"Yes?" She licked her lips and inhaled a deep breath to brace herself.

"If you'd like, you can come down to pick up the approved application. Or I can give you the basics over the phone and you can drop by anytime at your convenience."

"I guess I'd like to know now." She'd like to be able to make some concrete plans.

He ran through a whole string of numbers,

which she jotted down as fast as she could. Then came the bottom line. The amount the bank would be willing to loan her.

The number stunned her. She sat down hard on a kitchen chair. "Why is it so low? I'm sure I have a good credit rating." She hadn't had time to default on her credit cards, which she'd switched to her name after Raymond's death.

"I'm afraid much of your credit rating is related to your late husband's record, not yours."

"But I was the one who paid the bills for him and handled the accounts." Except for those bills he'd run up courting his various paramours, which he'd taken care of through a separate account unknown to her until after his death.

"I'm sure that's true, Ms. Townsend. I talked with Adam this morning. He had very high praise for you as his bookkeeper. But the truth is, you also don't have a steady income."

"I receive my husband's monthly death benefits and Social Security for my child. I know I'll be able to get a regular job after I'm settled in a new place. If not, I may run a bookkeeping service of my own." The threat of panic raised her voice.

"I know this result is disappointing for you."

"To say the least!" She ran her fingers through her hair. The Jackson house was now out of the question. What would that leave her with?

"If I may suggest, you could temporarily rent

a place in the area. This time of year, there are a good many excellent rentals available. Then, as you continue to establish your own credit and find employment, you could look forward to buying a house in a few months. Perhaps by next summer."

"Next—" The word stuck in her throat. "That would mean moving my daughter three times within one year. I need for her to be in a place where's she's comfortable and secure. I can't willy-nilly jump from house to house when she's still emotionally fragile as a result of her father's death."

"I am terribly sorry, Ms. Townsend. As you know, the mortgage market has changed considerably in the past few years. Things are much tighter now than they once were. We're very cautious about making loans these days."

"I see." She bit her lip. Now they decided to be cautious after the mess of the housing crash. A crash that had already cost her when she hadn't been able to get top dollar for the house in Seattle.

"If you'd like to come into the bank, I'd be happy to discuss this with you at length."

But he wouldn't change his mind. That was obvious by his tone.

"Thank you for calling, Mr. Muskie. I'll be in touch." She snapped the phone shut and put her head in her hands. Tears burned in her eyes. *Dear God, what am I going to do? I need Your help.*

She felt a tug on her sleeve.

"Mommy? Why are you crying?"

"Oh, sweetie." She tugged Raeanne into her arms and hugged her hard. "Mommy's not really crying. I just got something in my eyes that made them sting. I'm all right." She blinked away her tears but not her worries.

She'd badly overestimated the amount of money a bank would loan her. The only thing left to do was downsize her expectations. Look for something smaller, less expensive, most likely not located in as good a neighborhood as she had hoped.

Her determination to own her own home, to have a settled place for Raeanne, hadn't changed. Her last choice would be to rent.

She prayed it wouldn't come to that.

As soon as she could, Janelle called Sharon to tell her she'd have to start over, looking at homes with a much lower price tag. Unfortunately, Sharon was booked all weekend with an out-of-town couple looking for a vacation home in the area. Janelle's house hunting would have to wait until Monday.

Later in the day, Adam found her working at her laptop at the kitchen table.

"What's up?" He grabbed a soda from the refrigerator and popped the top.

"I'm looking at real-estate listings, the cheaper the better."

"Muskie couldn't get you a decent loan? I talked to him this morning. He promised to try."

She lifted her gaze to meet his. "I know. I appreciate your effort, but apparently you don't have as much pull with the bank as you thought you did. Rules for making loans have tightened up, according to Mr. Muskie."

"Yeah, he said something about that." He slid onto the chair next to her. "So what are you going to do? Put Sharon back to work showing you properties?"

"She's not available this weekend. Which is why I'm checking the listings myself. At least I can do a drive-by and eliminate those that don't come close to what I'm looking for."

"Tell you what." He downed a gulp of soda then set the can on the table. "I can't take off work tomorrow. But if you can wait until Sunday, we can do the drive-bys after church. How does that sound?" He reached for her hand and gave it a squeeze.

She held on tight. "I like the idea of you being with me. It's hard to make these decisions by myself."

"I'll help you. You won't be alone." His low, raspy voice wrapped around her, giving her a sense of comfort and security she desperately needed. But was that only an illusion? After she moved, would he still be there for her when she needed him?

* * *

That evening, Janelle settled down with a book while Adam worked on his reading lessons on the computer. She had to admire his effort. The past couple of nights, he'd worked his way through two lessons, not just one. Admirable.

A frown tugged at her forehead. Was he doing all that because of her? Or had he come to realize he needed to do it for himself? She knew he was still hiding his dyslexia from his friends.

If she were the only reason he was hurrying through the lessons, he'd come to resent her. Deep down he'd blame her for trying to change him instead of letting him be himself.

Before Raymond's death, her husband had hinted that it was her fault he spent so much time on the road visiting other universities. Was that just his excuse for having affairs with young coeds?

Or had she really failed him as a wife? Pressured him too hard? Tried to change his behavior?

She closed the book and rubbed her temple with her fingertips.

Raeanne's therapist in Seattle had told Janelle that both parties in a marriage carried some of the responsibility for its failure. Hurt as Janelle had been by the revelations of Raymond's infidelity, she hadn't given any credence to the therapist's comment.

Now she did.

What part of the failure of their marriage had

been hers? And how could she avoid damaging a future relationship in the same way?

No easy answers came to her.

After church on Sunday, they picked up some lunch at the Pee Wee Drive-In, which the girls loved. Despite clouds that threatened rain, they took their lunches to the municipal park, where they found a table and enjoyed their impromptu picnic. After giving the girls a chance to run off some of their pent-up energy, they were off to check out the houses for sale that Janelle thought were worth seeing.

Sitting in the front seat of the truck, she got out her notes. "I tried to organize things so we weren't running back and forth all over the county."

"Good idea." He turned the key in the ignition. "Where to first?"

"There are two houses in a small residential tract north of Main Street off of Pine. One of them is bank owned. Guess it was foreclosed." She hated that she had a chance to take advantage of someone else's loss, but this was no time for her social conscience to click on. If she didn't buy the house, someone else would.

"We're on our way." He pulled out of the parking lot onto Main Street. "What's the place like?"

She checked her notes. "Two bedrooms, one and a half baths, carport. On a quiet street."

"You'd probably want to enclose the carport. Winters here aren't as bad as some places in Montana, but it's still cold enough that the lake freezes over."

She shivered. "Not exactly Seattle weather."

"Lots more sunshine, though."

True. Clear skies and clean air. She liked that a lot.

When they stopped in front of the house, Hailey said, "It looks like a doll house."

It did—a doll house on a small lot that hadn't seen an occupant or a lawn mower the entire summer. Broken lawn furniture, chunks of wallboard and other trash were piled by the side of the house.

They all clambered out of the truck. The girls raced up to the front porch to peer in the window.

"Oh, ick!" Hailey cried. "It's a mess in there."

Janelle looked through the window. Just like the outside, the inside was a disaster. Janelle's heart sank. No question—either the former owners or transients had vandalized the place. The carpet had been torn up. Boxes were strewn about, and a hole had been punched in the wallboard beside the brick fireplace.

Surely she could do better than this.

Raeanne tugged on her hand. "I don't like this place."

"Neither do I, sweetie. We'll find something better." She glanced around the unkempt yard.

Her gaze landed on a gnarly old apple tree. "Hey, the house does have one redeeming feature—a crab-apple tree. Let's pick a few. I'll add them to the wreath on the front door."

The girls scurrying to gather some apples lightened the mood by the time they returned to the truck and drove on to the next house on Janelle's list.

Three drive-bys later they stopped in front of a small log cabin. A non-native maple tree in the yard was beginning to change color. A row of cypress trees formed a windscreen on one side of the house.

"What does it say about this place?" Adam asked.

"Two bedrooms, one bath and a loft. They call it a 'cozy vacation home.'"

Adam lifted his brows. "You want to take a closer look?"

"Might as well. It looks better than the others we've seen." Cozy was good, she told herself. She could raise Raeanne in a cozy house. Unfortunately, the image that came to her was Adam's house, which was far larger than this cabin but still cozy in its own way. Unfortunately, Adam's house did not appear on her list of possibilities.

Maybe she should have stayed in Seattle. She and Raymond had had a nice house not far from the university. But that place was filled with sad memories for both Janelle and Raeanne. To compound her problems, he had refinanced the house a couple of years ago to put money in an investment that he'd claimed couldn't fail, until it did. After she sold the house, she was sure that that cash would serve as an adequate down payment for a new house.

A misjudgment on her part.

A few drops of rain spattered down on Janelle's head as she looked in the windows of the cozy cabin. Though small, it appeared neat and livable. Still, her stomach twisted with disappointment. A dream lost.

By the time they got home, the rain was falling steadily and looked as if it would last awhile. The girls and Janelle were playing a board game. Adam decided to work on his reading lessons at the computer.

He brought up the program and stared unfocused at the screen. He didn't want Janelle and Rae living in that tiny cabin. They deserved something bigger. More in keeping with what they were used to.

Something like his house.

He clicked on the next lesson in sequence. He had to quit thinking about Janelle living with him permanently. That would mean marriage. Why would a woman like Janelle even consider marrying a garage mechanic who couldn't read worth beans?

Except now he could follow the ever-cheerful Ollie the Owl's instructions to pick out the words starting with *B: Boy, Box, Buy, But.* The letters were finally beginning to make sense. In the lessons, at least. He hadn't tried reading anything else yet. He figured he was a long way from being ready for prime-time reading.

Hailey popped up on the chair next to him. "Can I help you with your homework?"

He angled a glance in her direction. "I thought you were playing a game with Janelle and Rae."

She shrugged. "I went bankrupt. Raeanne beat the socks off me."

His lips twitched with a smile. "Ah. Tough competition, huh?"

She grinned. "Sometimes I let her win," she whispered. "Like Mom used to let me win."

He gave her a one-arm hug. "Good for you."

"I wish she could live here forever. She needs a big sister to watch out for her and teach her stuff."

Just how did Hailey expect him to arrange that? "She's got her mom. Janelle can teach her what she needs to know."

"But Janelle's old. She can't remember what it's like to be a little kid."

He sputtered a laugh. "You do know I'm older than she is, don't you?"

"That's my point, Dad. Raeanne needs someone like me who knows about kid stuff. And I..." She turned her head away, but not before Adam caught the glimmer of tears in her eyes. "I need a mom who can teach me grown-up girl stuff."

He felt as if he'd been sucker punched. He knew Hailey missed her mother, but he hadn't realized how much. Or that she was on the lookout for a replacement mom. Someone like Janelle.

Chapter Sixteen

On Monday, Janelle took Raeanne for her checkup with Dr. McCandless, a longtime pediatrician in Bear Lake. She was given a clean bill of health, both for her head injury and for enrolling in kindergarten. At lunchtime they all celebrated with root-beer floats.

When Tuesday rolled around, Adam found himself under an old Chevy that leaked oil. He hadn't made much progress finding the leak. All he could think about was that Janelle was off with Sharon. House hunting in Polson this afternoon. The girls had gone to a movie matinee with one of Hailey's friends and her mother, who had promised to keep a close eye on Raeanne.

Janelle was going to make a decision soon. School registration started next Monday. She wanted to list her new *permanent* address.

What was the big deal? She could use his address just as well. Nobody would care.

He lay there thinking about the smell of grease and oil that was so much a part of his life. Lisa had never cared.

Granted he cleaned up as best he could when he went in to dinner. But he doubted he washed off all the scent of the garage. The smell of how he made his living. Hardly an enticing aftershave aroma.

Janelle had never said a word about his smell. He wondered how she felt about it. And him.

Somebody kicked the bottom of his shoes, which were sticking out from under the car.

"You gone to sleep under there, boss?"

Adam winced. "No, I'm not asleep. I'm trying to find the leak."

Vern grabbed hold of his legs and pulled him and the creeper out from under the car. "Hey, cut that out!"

"You been acting funny for two days. Like you got a bellyache or something. You shoulda been able to fix that leak in fifteen minutes. You been under there for an hour. What's goin' on?"

Adam struggled to his feet and wiped his hands on a blue cloth. "None of your business, that's what."

"We got cars stacked up waitin' to get fixed. You're gonna ruin your business if you keep actin' this way." Vern narrowed his pale blue eyes and wiped the back of his hand across his mouth. "If I didn't know better, I'd say you was lovesick."

Adam took a step back and collided with the car. Sweat broke out on his forehead. "You don't know what you're talking about."

"I'm not so sure about that. Seems like that pretty little lady and her daughter's been hanging around here for more'n three weeks now. A man could get used to a thing like that."

"You're out of line, Vern. She's out hunting a house to buy right now. Soon as she finds something she likes, she's gone." A burning sensation scorched a hole in his stomach.

"And I'm guessing you'll be one sick puppy when she up and leaves."

"Tell you what, old man." He slammed the wiping cloth onto the concert floor. "You're so smart, you get under there and fix that leak. I've got other work to do."

He marched into his office and shut the door. Something he never did. Since the office was all glassed in, closing the door didn't keep nosy folks from watching him anyway. Keeping an eye on him and coming up with too many questions.

He switched on the computer. The truth was, he'd been in a blue funk since Sunday afternoon. Hailey wanted a mother. He wanted…what he couldn't have.

These had been the shortest three weeks of his

life. And yet he felt as if he'd known Janelle forever. After she moved out, she'd only come around when there was some bookkeeping to do. Maybe a couple of mornings a week.

No more sitting out on the deck or stargazing with her. No chance for sharing hot chocolate on a snowy winter night. No more sitting around the table eating the meal she'd cooked and helping her clean up after dinner.

He yanked open the file drawer. All those ridiculous red, green and blue file tabs mocked him. She'd created a system she thought he could handle. A system any five-year-old would understand.

Yeah, he got it. She thought he was about as smart as your average five-year-old.

"You're a genius when it comes to fixing cars," she had said.

That sure hadn't been true today.

By the time Janelle got home, Adam had managed to rouse himself out of his dark mood enough to install an oil filter in a SUV.

"Aren't the girls home yet?" she asked as she walked into the garage. She'd worn tan slacks and a peach sweater for her house-hunting efforts. Under the overhead lights, the outfit made her hair shimmer with streaks of red.

"They should be back soon. I imagine they went for ice-cream cones after the show."

"So much for having an appetite for dinner," she said with a wry smile.

"How'd it go in Polson?"

Her shrug was less than enthusiastic. "We saw a couple of houses that would do. But I'd still rather live here. In Bear Lake, I mean."

Had that been a slip of the tongue? *Here,* meaning at his house?

"I think I'm going to settle on the cozy log cabin we saw on Sunday. It has good year-round insulation and the school bus stops reasonably close. Sharon's going to talk to the owners. They live in Billings. I gather the wife's health isn't too good, so they haven't used the cabin in a couple of years."

"They'd be glad to get it off their hands, I guess." He looked back at the oil filter and twisted a nut down extra tight. Somebody would have a hard time getting that nut off next time they wanted to change the filter.

"I'm going to go collapse for a few minutes until the girls get home. I'll see you for dinner."

"Yeah, I'll be there." He braced his hands on the SUV's fender and drew a shaky breath. It wouldn't be long now before she'd be gone.

Better start getting used to it now, guitar boy.

His mood was still sour when he went to the Rotary meeting the next day. He shook hands with his friends, endured their jovial back slaps and good humor, but his heart wasn't in it.

Charlie sat next to him during lunch. "You look like someone died. Are your folks okay?"

"I guess. I haven't talked to them in a couple of weeks." Longer than that, he realized with a rush of guilt. Maybe he'd call tonight. But what could he say? He had a beautiful woman living in Grandma's cottage and he didn't want her to move out? That would get his mother on the next flight to Montana. Probably to help with the wedding plans. A wedding that was as unlikely as Bear Lake freezing over in July.

"Then what's going on? You sick or something?"

He wanted to tell Charlie to lay off him, but he was a good friend. They'd been buddies for a long time. No reason to bite off his head like he had Vern's yesterday. For which he'd apologized this morning.

"I guess I'm just tired."

"Maybe you need a vacation. I could use one, too. We could both close up shop this weekend. Leave the kids with somebody and go up north. Do some hiking and fishing. The tourists are beginning to thin out now."

Adam raised his brows. Under normal circumstances he might do just that. But his life didn't seem normal at the moment. "Maybe in September when the kids are settled in school."

Charlie cut into the sauce-covered chicken breast on his plate. "Guess that'd be better."

Adam had eaten about all the chicken and julienned squash he could gag down when Joshua Higgins, dressed as always in a suit and tie, called the meeting to order. He went through the usual run of announcements, pointed out that it was Harry's birthday, which caused him to drop a five-dollar bill in the health-and-welfare kitty, to the roar of much good-natured laughter.

"Now then, folks," Joshua said. "We've got a problem. Our nominating committee has come up with a full slate of officers for the coming year except for one rather important slot. No one has agreed to serve as president."

Adam tried to shrink into his chair.

"Owen, would you please present the report from the nominating committee," Joshua said.

Owen stood at his place across the room. He thanked his fellow committee members and listed those who had agreed to be nominated for the various club offices.

"We on the committee had made a unanimous choice for who we wanted to see as president next year. Unfortunately, he declined to accept the invitation. Without a very good reason, I should add."

Adam sank down even farther.

"According to our rules, in the absence of any

candidate for an elective position, we can nominate someone from the floor. The chair will now entertain nominations."

Immediately, Charlie stood. "I nominate the committee's unanimous choice for president, Adam Hunter."

The members cheered and applauded.

Adam clinched his fists, ready to punch out his buddy. A muscle in his jaw flexed. "I told you I don't want the job and won't take it."

"You're the guy everyone wants. Step up to the plate, man."

Adam stood and threw back his chair. "Like I told the committee, the answer is no."

Voices all around him started asking why not. Telling him that he'd be great as president. Calling him a chicken.

His instinct to fight or flee kicked in. He whirled and marched to the door. He wasn't going to stay around to listen to their catcalls. Listen to them make him the butt of their jokes.

He reached the door. The members had fallen into stunned silence. In that silence he heard Janelle's voice: *"They'd understand if you told them the truth."*

Slowly he turned back to the meeting. His heart beating hard, he stood at the end of the table, taking in these men and women who had been his friends. Most were older than him by a dozen or more years. A few were younger. None had been his classmates who had witnessed his failures in school time and again. They were friends who respected him. Who deserved the truth.

But would they really understand?

He cleared his throat. "The fact is, I'm not qualified for the job." Several members started to speak, but he held up his hand asking for quiet. "The president has a lot of jobs to do. A lot of those jobs involve, one way or another, being able to read and write." The lump in his throat persisted despite his effort to clear it away. "I can't read and write. I'm dyslexic."

No one spoke. There wasn't a whisper in the room. He imagined whatever respect he'd built in the past thirty-plus years, he'd shattered in one single truthful moment.

He hung his head. "I'm sorry."

He turned to leave again. Charlie stopped him.

"Don't go." He joined Adam at the door. "We didn't know."

"Now you do."

"Now we can make some accommodation. Make it work with you as president."

A bitter laugh escaped Adam's chest. A circus horse who could read would work fine.

Charlie looped his arm around Adam's shoulders. "If Adam had an assistant who could handle the paperwork, he could lead us as president. He's got the ideas that will make this club a leader in the Rotary nation. I volunteer to be his assistant."

Stunned, Adam shook his head in dismay. "You're crazy."

Apparently the membership didn't agree. "Let's hear it for President Hunter!"

"Hear! Hear!"

"I move we cast a unanimous vote for Adam and the entire slate of officers."

"Aye, aye."

The treasurer-elect joined Charlie and Adam. "I'll coach you on the budget. You're smart, Adam. You won't need to read it to understand the numbers."

The secretary-elect and program chair added their support for Adam.

"There you have it, ladies and gentlemen." Joshua pounded his gavel on the podium. "Our slate of officers for the coming year."

Charlie pushed Adam in the direction of the podium. "Get up there, man, and tell us what a great year we're going to have. I may be your assistant, but I'm sure not going to give your speeches for you."

Staggered by the outpouring of support, their friendship and respect, Adam made his way to the podium.

Joshua shook his hand. "You'll do fine, son. We're all proud of you and what you've accomplished." He handed Adam the gavel.

Conflicting emotions left him speechless. Him? President of the Rotary? That was the biggest joke he'd ever heard. Yet, here he stood, gavel in hand.

He banged it on the podium. "All right, you guys. And gals." He nodded toward the two female members. "You asked for this. My first item of business is to fine you all a buck for not listening to me when I said no. Charlie, pass the kitty. Make sure they all ante up. You first."

Laughing, they all dug out their wallets.

As he looked around the room, Adam didn't know whether to thank the Lord for this opportunity or to tell God he'd blown it. Either way, Adam vowed to do the best he could to make the Bear Lake Rotary the most outstanding club in the country. Maybe even the world.

If he succeeded, he'd have to give Janelle the credit. Without her, he never would have had the courage to tell the truth.

Rather than going back to work when he got home, Adam went in search of Janelle. He didn't know if he was proud or scared about being the Rotary president, but he wanted to share the news with her.

He found her working at the dining-room table.

She'd spread the floor plan of the log cabin on the table and was arranging cutout bits of paper representing pieces of furniture in the various rooms.

The muscles in his throat contracted and he swallowed hard. "Looks like you're doing some serious planning."

She glanced up and he noticed she was wearing the rose necklace he'd given her. He swallowed a second time. Would she remember him each time she wore the necklace? Or would he be forgotten as soon as she went out the door?

"I'm trying to figure out how the furniture I have in storage in Seattle will fit in such a small house. Basically, the answer is it won't. Or at least I'll have a lot of stuff to get rid of."

"That's too bad."

"Hmm." She cocked her head. "Is something wrong?"

"No, not really. It's just that I told the Rotary Club why I couldn't be their president. That I'm dyslexic."

Her eyes widened. The hint of a smile tilted her lips momentarily and then she frowned. "How did they react?"

"They were pretty quiet at first. Then Charlie Brooks volunteered to be my assistant to read stuff. So they went ahead and elected me president."

"Oh, Adam…" She leaped up from her chair and threw her arms around his neck.

He held her close, inhaling her floral-scented shampoo.

"I'm so proud of you. I know how hard it was for you to admit—"

He didn't want her to talk anymore. So he stopped her with a kiss. The kiss he'd wanted to repeat since that first time in the lobby of the IRS building. A kiss that he wanted to continue for as long as possible. And never let her go.

He shifted his position to hold her more tightly.

Slowly she pushed away, letting her hands slide down his arms. The gold flecks in her brown eyes glittered like sunshine.

"Congratulations." Her voice had a husky quality he'd never heard.

"Thanks. It's all your doing, you know. Without you, I never would have told them." Granted, his knees were still knocking and his stomach was unsettled, but the ordeal was over. They all knew the truth now. The town would know soon enough.

A tiny frown pulled her brows together. "You're happy you told them, aren't you?"

He nodded. "It's better not to have to keep it a secret anymore."

A bell ringing out on the deck caused them both to look in that direction. The girls were out there.

He dropped his arms from around Janelle. She took a step back.

"What are the girls up to?" he asked.

"Hailey decided she should get Rae used to going to school. She got out some of her old coloring books and the whiteboard she keeps in her room. She's the teacher and Rae is her student."

"Cute."

"It is." Janelle smiled fondly as she watched the girls. "She has Raeanne writing her letters and her numbers and coloring inside the lines. When they get tired of that, Hailey rings a bell for recess."

"My favorite period, recess."

"I bet you were the best dodgeball player in the school."

He had been. In order not to be teased for being so "dumb" in class, he had to be the best fighter, too.

Today he hadn't had to fight. The class dunce had just been elected president of the class.

It felt plenty good.

Janelle had felt plenty good in his arms. But he didn't know how to keep her there.

Chapter Seventeen

Later that evening the phone rang. Automatically, Janelle picked up the extension on the kitchen counter.

"Hello." There was silence for a moment, long enough to make her think it was a telemarketer calling.

"I'm not sure I have the right number," a woman said at last. "Is Adam there?"

She shot a glance toward Adam, who was relaxing on the couch and watching a baseball game on television. "Yes, just a moment please." She covered the mouthpiece on the phone. "It's for you. A woman." A woman with a very pleasant voice, Janelle thought with an unwelcome spurt of jealously.

"Thanks." Not appearing either concerned or delighted, he walked over to the counter and took the phone. "Hello…Hey, Mom, I was thinking about you this morning. Sorry I haven't called lately."

Janelle left the kitchen, scolding herself for feeling so relieved. Even if it had been an old girlfriend, or a new one, there was no reason for her to become jealous. She and Adam had no agreement beyond bookkeeping services. Their kiss this afternoon—and the one at the IRS office—didn't mean they had a romantic relationship. Certainly there'd been no talk of a commitment. Rightfully so. She had to get her own life settled before she could even consider such a thing.

She had no claim on Adam.

"No, Mom, I'm just doing her a favor," she heard Adam explain. "She brought her car in after an accident and needed a place for her and her daughter to stay for a few days."

It sounded as though Mom had a lot of questions about the woman who had answered the phone. Janelle couldn't blame her.

She picked up the book she'd been reading earlier but couldn't help hearing his side of the conversation. Evidently, since his wife died, he hadn't generally had a woman in the house. Which was a relief to know, of course, but none of Janelle's business.

It was also nice to hear his love for his mother in his voice. Some men weren't that attached to their parents, often ignoring them or carrying on feuds over past insults, real or imagined. Adam would never be one of those men.

As his conversation began to wind down, she concentrated on her book. A complicated mystery, she'd lost track of who the characters were and their respective motives for murdering a stranger who had come to town. She turned back a few pages to pick up the story thread she'd lost.

Adam hung up the phone. "That was my mother."

She glanced up from the book. "I gathered as much."

"Dad's off with his astronomy buddies. I think she was feeling lonely."

Nodding, Janelle said, "I guess having a woman answer your phone surprised her."

He stuck his fingertips in the back pockets of his jeans. "Don't worry about it. I explained things."

"I heard." Heard him backpedaling as fast as he could to deny any romantic connection between them. Which was the proper thing to do.

"She's okay. I think you'd like her."

"I'm sure I would." His mother had, after all, raised Adam into a fine, hardworking, generous man who was an excellent father. Those were admirable traits.

Traits that could make a woman fall in love with him even when she shouldn't. She glanced down at her book, where she found that the words had blurred.

He picked up the TV remote. "I'd better get to work on my reading lesson. You want the TV on?"

"No, I'll read for a while. I'm not much of a baseball fan. You go ahead."

Janelle wondered if he'd miss her when she moved into the new house. She imagined the quiet in that small, cozy cabin and knew she'd miss him. And Hailey. The noise. The laughter. Knowing there were people other than her daughter nearby whom she cared about very much.

Giving up all pretense of reading, she closed her book. She was making herself maudlin about leaving Adam's house and moving into her own place. That wasn't how she imagined it would be when she set off from Seattle with her grand plan of starting a new life.

She squeezed the book in her hands. *Please, Lord, help me through this. Guide me. Help me to walk the path You have planned for me and give me peace in the decisions I have to make. Thy will be done. Amen.*

All the next day, Adam was a wreck. He'd never dropped so many screwdrivers and wrenches in his life. Nuts and bolts slipped through his fingers as if they were covered in grease.

He was going to lose Janelle. Sure, he could call her for a date after she moved out. Court her properly. Take her out to dinner. Even arrange for playdates for the girls.

But it wouldn't be the same without her here. In his home. In his life every day.

Yet he had no right to ask her to stay. Why would she want to? She'd said all along she planned to start over in a new home with Raeanne. That was her goal. To establish her independence and begin again.

She had every right to build the life she wanted.

He didn't have the right to stop her. Even if that was a possibility, which he doubted.

At dinner that evening, Janelle dropped the bomb he'd been dreading.

"Sharon called this afternoon. She's talked with the owners of the cabin. Everything looks good. I'm going over to Sharon's office first thing in the morning to sign the official offer on the house."

The mac and cheese she'd prepared for dinner turned into a stone in Adam's stomach. "If that's what you've decided, sounds good." The stone grew into a boulder. He put his fork down.

"Are you really going to move into that cabin?" Hailey asked, a tiny whine in her voice.

"That's the plan." Janelle spoke almost too brightly. With too much enthusiasm. "Sharon thinks she can get a short escrow. Maybe as short as fifteen days."

"But that's only two weeks," Hailey complained. Her lower lip quivered.

Adam's lip would have quivered, too, except he was biting down hard to keep from begging Janelle to stay. *Don't leave me! Don't leave us!*

Raeanne jumped down from her chair. She came around the table and gave Hailey a hug. "Don't cry. Mommy says we can come visit you. I'll bring Kitty Cat with me. I promise."

"But I don't want you to go." Hailey broke into sobs. The girls rocked back and forth in each other's arms.

Adam was pretty choked up himself. When he looked at Janelle, he thought she was, too. Her lips pursed together. Tears shimmered in her eyes. She was a woman. She ought to know how to deal with two crying females. He sure didn't.

"Girls, I want you to finish your dinner." She glanced at him, but he couldn't offer any help. "We have ice cream for dessert. We can talk about the move tomorrow after I've seen Sharon. Now is the time to eat."

Raeanne trudged back to her chair. Instead of sitting down, however, she put her arms around her mother. "I don't want to go, Mommy. I want to stay here with Hailey and Adam."

Janelle squeezed her eyes shut. A tear clung to the tips of her eyelashes. "We'll talk tomorrow, sweetie. Everything's going to be all right. You'll see."

Adam wasn't so sure.

After Janelle and Raeanne left to go to the cottage for the night, Adam sat on the couch thinking. He leaned his elbows on his thighs, his hands clasped together between his knees. He worried a hangnail on his thumb.

Hailey was already in bed. He didn't think he'd be able to sleep if he called it a night.

How could he get Janelle to stay with him? Did he even have a right to ask? She'd been married. Maybe she wasn't ready to try it again. Not so soon after she lost her husband, anyway. Although he'd gathered her relationship with her husband had lacked something. Something he wanted to give her. His undying love.

He couldn't get over the fact that Janelle had encouraged him to open up to his friends and his daughter, tell them about his dyslexia. Lisa had loved him but had always wanted him to keep his disability a secret.

Janelle genuinely accepted him.

But could she love him?

He got up and walked out onto the deck. The temperature had dropped into the high fifties. Fall was coming fast. A high overcast blocked all but the brightest stars. The North Star. The points of Pegasus. Lyra.

How come he could read the stars but he couldn't read words on the page? He couldn't read Janelle, either.

What was she thinking over in the cottage? No light showed around the edges of the window. She was probably already in bed dreaming about her new home.

He kicked at a pile of stones the girls had left on the deck. He had to do something. He couldn't let her go without at least trying.

But not face-to-face. He didn't think he could stand to see rejection in her expressive brown eyes.

Back inside, he went into the kitchen. Lisa had always kept a pad of paper and some pencils in one of the drawers. He yanked it open and pawed through a collection of junk. A box of rubber bands. A sheet of thumbtacks. Glue and scissors.

Uncovering the pad and pencils, he placed them on the kitchen table and sat down. This might be the dumbest thing he'd ever done. Writing a love letter when he was still barely able to read. Or write.

He licked the tip of the pencil.

Dere Janie...

After a restless night, Janelle dressed for her trip to the Realtor. She wished she were more excited about this step in her life and not having so many second thoughts.

"You ready for breakfast?"

Raeanne, sitting on the edge of the bed with Kitty Cat, had one monster of a puffed-out lower lip. Poor kid. She was as distraught about the house Janelle had picked out as her mother was. Or, more likely, she hadn't adjusted to leaving Hailey. And Adam.

If truth be known, Janelle hadn't adjusted, either. The loss of the closeness she'd developed with Adam, so quickly, made her heart ache.

"If you don't tuck your lip back inside your mouth, a big old fly is going to sit on it," Janelle teased.

Raeanne sucked her lip back into place. "Do we have to move?"

"We can't stay here forever, sweetie. This is Adam's house, not ours."

She canted her head toward Janelle. "Hailey said if you and her daddy got married, we could all stay here together."

Heat rushed to Janelle's cheeks. Children certainly knew how to get to the crux of the matter. And they lived in a fantasy world of happily-ever-afters, a world that didn't really exist. Not based on her experience. Dreams didn't always come true.

Seeing no good way to respond to Rae's comment, she smoothed her hand over her daughter's hair. "You know how much I love you, don't you?"

She looked up with her big brown eyes. "More than the moon and the stars and the sky."

"That's right." Janelle had been repeating those words to Raeanne ever since she'd been a baby, and her love for Rae hadn't change a bit in all those years. Nor would it in a hundred more years. "Let's go have some breakfast."

To her surprise, although the coffee was ready, there was no sign that Adam had eaten any breakfast. She couldn't hear the shower running. He wasn't out on the dock fussing with his boat.

She concluded he'd either had an early appointment or had gone out to the garage to get some work done.

She poured herself some coffee and got down some cereal for Raeanne. About then Hailey shuffled into the kitchen sporting serious bedhead. She went directly to the cupboard to get her own cereal.

"Good morning, Hailey. You look like you're still sleepy."

She made a nonverbal grunting response as she got the milk out of the refrigerator.

"Do you know where your dad is?"

Hailey lifted one shoulder. "In the garage, I guess."

So much for scintillating morning conversation.

It wasn't often Hailey's bubbly personality went into hiding.

They ate in silence; the girls their cereal and juice; Janelle, toast and coffee. Not even Kitty Cat seemed able to stir up any interest from the girls despite her best efforts at frolicking around the kitchen.

When they were finished, Janelle rinsed the dishes and put them in the dishwasher.

"I'm going to make sure Adam's all right with my leaving you girls here with him. Then I'll go on to the Realtor's office." She kissed both girls and got only a lukewarm response. "Behave yourselves. I love you."

Her determination to buy the cabin faltered. The girls both looked so unhappy, particularly Raeanne. Maybe she ought to keep hunting for a better house. Or even find one to rent nearby so the girls could see each other more often.

But kindergarten enrollment was next Monday. School started for all the students on Wednesday. There'd be little chance for the girls to get together. Besides, Hailey would be with her friends at school. Hanging out with a five-year-old might not have the same appeal as during the summer when friends were out of town or hard to reach.

"I'll be back soon," she promised. Squaring her shoulders, she went out the door.

Adam was leaning against her car.

Janelle's footsteps faltered. "Is something wrong? I missed you at breakfast."

He pushed away from the car. "Nothing's wrong." Although his tone suggested something was amiss. "I wanted to give you something before you left to see Sharon."

"Oh?" Puzzled, she tried to read his expression and got nowhere. "I'm leaving the girls here. I should be back soon. Is that okay?"

"Sure. I'll keep an eye out. Better than I did last time." He handed her an envelope.

The exterior was blank. No name on it. "What's this?"

His gaze skittered away. "It's a note."

She started to open the envelope.

"You don't have to read it now. Maybe when you get to Sharon's office."

How odd. The contents of the envelope didn't feel thick. A single piece of paper. Why did he want her to wait? she wondered.

He opened the car door for her. Filled with curiosity about the letter, she slid inside. He closed the door after her and stepped away. What in the world was he up to?

Realizing she wasn't going to get an answer from Adam, or until she opened the envelope, she turned the key in the ignition, shifted into gear and drove out onto the highway. Traffic was light through town, although she noticed the parking lot at Pine Tree Diner was filled with cars. She still hadn't had a chance to try their potato pancakes. Maybe this weekend.

Sharon's car was parked in the Lake Country Real Estate lot when she arrived. Janelle pulled in next to it.

With a few minutes left before her appointment, Janelle decided to satisfy her curiosity. She ripped open the envelope and unfolded the single piece of white paper inside.

She drew in a quick breath as she read.

Dere Janie. Befor u buy a hous I need to tel u how I feel.

She placed her hand over her heart as though to slow its rapid pounding. His handwriting was no better than Raeanne's. His spelling was atrocious. But there was no doubt about it. Adam Hunter, who struggled to read and write at all, had written her a love letter.

I no I am just a mechanic an u ar smart an butiful. But no man could luv you more. I luv the way yor hair brushes yor sholders. I luv yor smil an the way u look at Rae with so much luv. I luv the sound of yor laufter.

Tears began to creep down Janelle's cheeks and drop on the note. She dragged in a shaky breath.

I luvd u when u fel out of the boat and could still laf.

An unexpected laugh escaped between her tears.

Most of al I luv al of u. I want to mary u and luv u the rest of my lif.
Adam.
P.S. I luv Rae to an want to be her daddy.

Janelle covered her mouth with her hand to stifle a sob. "I love you, too, Adam. With all my heart." Her voice shook.

Wiping her eyes, she started the car and wheeled out of the parking lot. She picked up her cell and punched in Sharon's number. Briefly she told the Realtor she wouldn't be making an offer on the house after all, promising to explain later.

She'd vowed not to get involved with another man until she'd gotten her own life and Raeanne's together. Apparently, her heart—and the Lord— had decided otherwise. There was nothing more she wanted than to marry Adam and share her life with him and the two beautiful girls they both loved.

Within minutes she was back home at the garage. She'd barely brought the car to a stop when she leaped out and ran into the garage.

"Adam!"

He looked up from his work in time to catch her when she flew into his arms.

She kissed him and held him. "I love you, Adam. With every ounce of my being, I love you and always will."

A smile tilted one corner of his lips. "My letter worked?"

"Oh, yes! Yes! I've been praying and hoping and wanting—"

"Then you'll marry me?"

"That's what I've been saying. Yes, I'll marry you. I can't wait to be Mrs. Adam Hunter."

"You changed your mind about getting your own place, starting over?"

"The only way I want to start over is with you."

He kissed her then, full on her lips, and her heart soared.

After what seemed like a delicious eternity, she broke the kiss. "There are a few things I have to tell you, though."

He cocked a brow.

"First of all, I never want to hear you refer to yourself as *just* a mechanic. You're a wonderful, wonderful mechanic who can fix anything on wheels, and everyone in town knows it."

"Okay." He grinned. "I can accept that."

"Furthermore I don't want you to change. I apologize for backing you into a corner and forcing you to learn how to read. Whether you can read or not, I love you exactly as you are. Exactly the way God made you. With all your goodness and loving heart and your dyslexia."

"That's good. But those internet lessons are helping. I'm reading better."

"I know. And I love you for that, too."

"Will you love me when I'm old and bald?"

She laughed a joyous sound. "Absolutely. Will you love me when I'm old and fat?"

"There'd be all the more of you to love, then."

He tugged her closer and she held on to him with all her strength and all the love she felt for him.

Behind them, Vern cleared his throat. "Guess you're too busy to take care of Mr. Rashmere's transmission right now."

A flush burned Janelle's cheeks. She tried to step away from Adam, but he kept his arms around her.

"You take care of Rashmere, Vern. We've got something else we have to do."

She gave him a questioning look.

"Let's go tell the girls. I think this news is exactly the thing to lift their spirits."

Janelle agreed. "You think it's okay if I use your

address when I enroll Raeanne in kindergarten? Even though we're not married yet."

"It's *our* address," he emphasized. "All four of us. And you can be sure you'll be my wife as soon as I can get the preacher over here to do the deed."

She laughed. "Maybe we shouldn't marry quite that fast. I imagine your parents would like to attend the service. And your brother."

"My mother would be here tomorrow if I told her we were getting married. Dad, too, if she had to drag him here."

Janelle imagined so. The thought of such loving parents becoming part of her life thrilled her and made her miss her mother and father all the more.

But now she'd have a true family of her own.

Arm in arm, they walked into the house to tell their two daughters that they were all going to be a family. A family filled with love, happiness and a shared future.

Thank You, Lord, for leading me to this wonderful man.

* * * * *

Dear Reader,

Over the years our family has enjoyed many camping and fishing trips to Montana. (I admit I need a little remedial help with my fly-fishing technique and I really don't look very stylish in waders.)

I'm fortunate to be able to "return" to Montana through my writing and recall the lovely sunsets, glistening clear lakes, wild animals strolling along the roadside and the restorative scent of clean air and pine and fir trees. I hope you've enjoyed visiting some of those same experiences through this story.

The hero of this book, Adam Hunter, has dyslexia. According to the International Dyslexia Association, as many as 15–20% of the population have some symptoms of dyslexia, including slow or inaccurate reading, poor spelling and writing, or mixing up similar words.

For purposes of this story, I compressed Adam's progress in learning to read as an adult. But there is help available for those who cannot read well, both online and through library and adult education programs.

Above all, a person who has dyslexia should not feel ashamed of his or her disability. As Janelle, our heroine, says of Adam, "God made you that way." An individual with reading problems can seek help to improve his or her reading skills without fear of blame or censure.

Meanwhile, I wish you...happy reading!

Charlotte Carter

Questions for Discussion

1. Did it surprise you that Janelle had moved away from her hometown after the death of her husband? Why or why not?

2. If you had fallen in love with someone who could not read, would that have bothered you? Why or why not?

3. Janelle and Adam's first kiss took place in a public place. How would you have felt about that?

4. Do you have friends or family members who are dyslexic? How do they cope with their dyslexia?

5. Does your school district have a reading specialist who works with students with reading difficulties? If not, have you or others in the community supported an effort to fund such a position?

6. What were your children's favorite picture books when they were young? What were yours?

7. Do you and your family enjoy camping and fishing? If so, where is your favorite spot to fish?

8. Have you ever visited Glacier National Park? If so, what impressed you the most?

9. What would it be like to live in a tourist town? Would you enjoy that?

10. Do you know any blended families with his and her children? What adjustments have the families had to make to live together in harmony?

11. Do you, or did you ever, sing in a church choir? What was that like?

12. What effect do you think Janelle's losing her parents before she was twenty had on her?

13. What difficulties do single parents face when raising a child on their own? Does it make a difference if the child is young or an adolescent? Boy or girl?

14. Have you ever written a love letter? Or received one? Have you saved those that you received?

15. Adam and Janelle are mature adults. What age do you think is a good age to get married? Why?

16. Do you think it would be easier for a single parent to raise a child of the same or opposite sex? Why?

LARGER-PRINT BOOKS!

**GET 2 FREE
LARGER-PRINT NOVELS
PLUS 2 FREE
MYSTERY GIFTS**

Larger-print novels are now available...

YES! Please send me 2 FREE LARGER-PRINT Love Inspired® novels and my 2 FREE mystery gifts (gifts are worth about $10). After receiving them, if I don't wish to receive any more books, I can return the shipping statement marked "cancel". If I don't cancel, I will receive 6 brand-new novels every month and be billed just $4.99 per book in the U.S. or $5.49 per book in Canada. That's a saving of at least 23% off the cover price. It's quite a bargain! Shipping and handling is just 50¢ per book in the U.S. and 75¢ per book in Canada.* I understand that accepting the 2 free books and gifts places me under no obligation to buy anything. I can always return a shipment and cancel at any time. Even if I never buy another book, the two free books and gifts are mine to keep forever.

122/322 IDN FEG3

Name	(PLEASE PRINT)
Address	Apt. #
City	State/Prov.	Zip/Postal Code

Signature (if under 18, a parent or guardian must sign)

Mail to the **Reader Service**:
IN U.S.A.: P.O. Box 1867, Buffalo, NY 14240-1867
IN CANADA: P.O. Box 609, Fort Erie, Ontario L2A 5X3

Not valid to current subscribers to Love Inspired Larger-Print books.

**Are you a current subscriber to Love Inspired books
and want to receive the larger-print edition?
Call 1-800-873-8635 or visit www.ReaderService.com.**

* Terms and prices subject to change without notice. Prices do not include applicable taxes. Sales tax applicable in N.Y. Canadian residents will be charged applicable taxes. Offer not valid in Quebec. This offer is limited to one order per household. All orders subject to credit approval. Credit or debit balances in a customer's account(s) may be offset by any other outstanding balance owed by or to the customer. Please allow 4 to 6 weeks for delivery. Offer available while quantities last.

Your Privacy—The Reader Service is committed to protecting your privacy. Our Privacy Policy is available online at www.ReaderService.com or upon request from the Reader Service.

We make a portion of our mailing list available to reputable third parties that offer products we believe may interest you. If you prefer that we not exchange your name with third parties, or if you wish to clarify or modify your communication preferences, please visit us at www.ReaderService.com/consumerschoice or write to us at Reader Service Preference Service, P.O. Box 9062, Buffalo, NY 14269. Include your complete name and address.

LILP11B

Love Inspired® SUSPENSE

RIVETING INSPIRATIONAL ROMANCE

Watch for our series of edge-
of-your-seat suspense novels.
These contemporary tales
of intrigue and romance
feature Christian characters
facing challenges to their faith...
and their lives!

AVAILABLE IN REGULAR & LARGER-PRINT FORMATS

For exciting stories that reflect traditional values,
visit:
www.ReaderService.com